BLUE
the
BRAVE

Alma Jordan lives on a farm in County Meath with her husband Mark and son Eamon. After a successful career in marketing and communications, she founded the award-winning social enterprise AgriKids in 2015 to spread the message of farm safety to children in a fun and engaging way.

Alma grew up on a farm in County Kildare, and the Hazel Tree Farm series features lots of real-life stories from her childhood, as well as moments shared by the children she meets through her work today.

HAZEL
tree
farm

BLUE
the
BRAVE

ALMA JORDAN

ILLUSTRATED BY MARGARET ANNE SUGGS

THE O'BRIEN PRESS
DUBLIN

DEDICATION

For Mark, Eamon and Benji.
And of course the 'Newbawns' from Hazelhatch.

ACKNOWLEDGMENTS

To my husband Mark for his support and advice on all things hen and
sheep (and coming soon, cows!). To Donie Anderson, my sheepdog
command advisor. Also to Nicola Reddy, who guided this newbie
every step of the way. To Kunak McGann and all at O'Brien Press,
especially Michael O'Brien, for making my dream come true.

First published 2023 by
The O'Brien Press Ltd,
12 Terenure Road East, Rathgar, Dublin 6, D06 HD27, Ireland.
Tel: +353 1 4923333; Fax: +353 1 4922777
E-mail: books@obrien.ie; Website: obrien.ie
The O'Brien Press is a member of Publishing Ireland.

ISBN: 978-1-78849-332-1

1 3 5 7 8 6 4 2
23 25 27 26 24

Printed in the UK by Clays Ltd, St Ives plc.

Blue the Brave receives financial
assistance from the Arts Council

Published in

CONTENTS

CHAPTER ONE: RAINBOW SPRINKLES   PAGE 6

CHAPTER TWO: THE BESTEST EGGS   16

CHAPTER THREE: AN UNWELCOME VISITOR   28

CHAPTER FOUR: TREATS & TRIALS   46

CHAPTER FIVE: LARRY'S (LITTLE) PRESENTS   60

CHAPTER SIX: OUTFOXED   72

CHAPTER SEVEN: STRONG STOCK   84

CHAPTER EIGHT: ALL SHEEPS AND SIZES   98

CHAPTER NINE: FLUFFBALLS   114

CHAPTER TEN: THE BIG DAY   132

Rainbow Sprinkles

'Peter! Peter! Peter!'

The chants from the crowd rang out across the stadium. Peter Farrelly, the world's most famous inventor, had done it – he had truly done it! Peter had created the Smart Cone, the world's first interactive, voice-controlled ice-cream cone. Holding it aloft to his adoring fans, Peter drew a finger to his lips. A *hussssssssh* descended on the crowd, the anticipation almost unbearable.

'Rainbow sprinkles,' Peter commanded in a deep, authoritative tone.

A rainbow arched over the cone, illuminating Peter's face in its multi-coloured splendour. As coloured droplets fell, the cone was sprinkled with tiny beads of candy colour.

'Marshmallows!' Peter boomed.

Tiny 'marshmallow' clouds appeared and hovered over the creamy cone, gently dotting fluffy puffs amongst the creamy swirls. The crowd was spellbound, in awe of this truly amazing invention.

'It is the most incredible thing I've ever seen,' said Mr Jenkins, Peter's fourth-class teacher.

'Peter will be a gazillionaire!' said Tommy Brennan, the most popular boy in St Brendan's National School.

'My brother is the greatest inventor ever!' replied Kate, Peter's little sister (who was quite a brainbox herself).

Peter raised his hand, and the bellowing crowd grew silent once more.

'And now for the grand finale,' he said, staring at the cone, with its delicious spray of sprinkles and marshmallows.

Peter blinked his eyes. The once-vanilla cone was now chocolate ... Blink! Now it was rocky road ... Blink! Now strawberry ... Blink, blink! Chocolate and vanilla!

His fans were on their feet, their applause and cheers almost deafening.

'Eat it! Eat it! Eat it!'

There was only one thing left for Peter to do now: have a taste of his truly glorious creation.

'Go on, Peter, take a big bite!' shouted Mr Jenkins.

'You can do it, Peter, I know you can!' Kate was jumping

up and down.

'You are truly the best, Peter Farrelly,' said Tommy Brennan, punching the air.

Peter brought the cone closer to his face. Little sticky ice-cream trails were trickling down the sides.

'Peter, Peter, Peter …' The crowd was growing restless, almost like a jungle tribe chanting to its leader.

Closer and closer …

Not long now until the creamy deliciousness was his and only his …

Closer and closer …

Peter stuck out his tongue. He was hardly able to wait a second more … Just a few millimetres …

Sluuuurrrpppppp!

Suddenly, something wet hit Peter's face.

Sluuuurrrpppppp, Sluuuurrrpppppp!

There it was again, and again. His face was soaking! Looking at his beautiful ice cream, Peter squealed in horror as a big tongue suddenly shot out of it. His amazing Smart Cone was licking his face, and what's more, it had two big eyes, one brown and one blue, and was covered in black fur.

AGGGGHHHHH! Peter sat bolt upright in his bed.

His amazing dream had been interrupted by Blue, his sheep-dog, who was licking her master's face to wake him up. Her long tongue went from chin to brow in one sloppy movement.

'Ahhhh, Blue, you ruined my dream!' wailed Peter.

Blue didn't care about any dream – she had to groom her young master and make sure he knew just how much she loved him. Her wet nose nuzzled under his chin, tickling him.

'Ok, I'm up, I'm up.' Peter rolled out of bed, wiping his face. 'There are less gross ways of waking someone up, you know!'

Satisfied that morning wash time was complete, Blue hopped off the bed and waited patiently for Peter to get dressed. Her tail thumped on the ground and her tongue lolled out of her mouth, at the ready should another wash and groom be required.

Peter lived at Hazel Tree Farm with his sister Kate, his mam and dad and of course Miss Blue the sheepdog. Even though Kate was two whole years younger than Peter, she was smarter than most other eight-year-olds and rarely had her head out of a book.

The Farrellys had always lived at Hazel Tree Farm, which had been a busy sheep farm going all the way back to Peter's great-great-grandfather. It was named after a lone hazel tree that had stood for a hundred years in the woods behind the meadow but came down in a storm on the night Blue was born. Afterwards, Dad placed an old wooden bench beside its stump, and it was everyone's favourite spot to sit and watch the lambs run around in the spring sunshine.

Peter and Kate's dad had grown up at Hazel Tree Farm too, and Peter's room was once Dad's room. He would often open the door of the wardrobe and shine a torch to the bottom corner where his dad had written, 'DAVID FARRELLY WOZ ERE FEB 1982'. He couldn't imagine his dad being ten years old, like him!

'I remember putting up posters of tractors and B.A. from *The A-Team*,' Dad told him one time, as they painted the bedroom walls in Peter's favourite colour, John Deere green. 'Your granny would get so cross when I used sticky tape because it tore the wallpaper.'

'What's a B.A.?' asked Peter. 'And who are *The A-Team*?'

Mam laughed as she laid sheets on the wooden floors to catch the drops of paint. 'It's a TV show from a VERY long time ago.' She smiled cheekily at Dad.

'Thanks, Marian,' Dad grumbled, pretending to be annoyed.

'It's a great room,' he continued. 'I always loved how the windows open up onto the main yard and you get the best view of the fields and woodland out back. I especially loved hearing the hens next door in Coopers' – their clucking would send me to sleep.'

Peter smiled. He loved that too.

'In fact,' said Dad, 'I think I used to hear things happening on the farm before my own dad did!'

Mam enjoyed hearing stories of Hazel Tree Farm in the old

days too. She knew David had had a very happy childhood here, and she wanted the same for her own young family.

Marian Farrelly also grew up on a farm, not too far away, and now she was a vet with a small-animal clinic at the back of Hazel Tree farmhouse. Her patients were mainly dogs and cats, with the occasional gerbil or hamster. One time she treated a budgie called Bertie, who had a very bad cold. Every time he sneezed, Bertie squawked 'Bless you! Bless you!', much to the amusement of Peter and Kate, who could hear him at the other end of the hall.

Behind the main house, there were acres of green fields and woodland. Most mornings, the children would sit at the kitchen table, positioning their bowls of cereal at the perfect angle so they could watch Dad working in the fields while munching their cornflakes. The animal sheds and outhouses were right beside the house, which made things easier during lambing season.

Lambing season, in early spring, was by far the busiest time of year at Hazel Tree Farm. No sooner was the Christmas tree put away than Dad was getting sheds ready for the impending new arrivals. Having the house close by meant he could quickly run in for a bucket of warm water or bring a sickly lamb into the kitchen, where Mam always had a basket set up next to the warm stove.

Over the years, the farm had grown as Mam and Dad added

more sheep. And with a growing flock, they had to add bigger sheds and secure more land. The fields provided grass for the sheep to graze on in the warmer months, and to make hay for winter when the fields got mucky and the grass more scarce.

You might think that the best thing about a growing farm was all the animals, but not for Peter. Nope! For Peter, having a growing farm also meant the need for … more machines!

Peter's *other* favourite thing about life on a farm was all the machinery. At different times of the year the countryside would hum with the sounds of busy farmers at work – ploughing in autumn, sowing in spring and harvesting throughout the summer. Soon, the countryside would be waking up after its winter slumber to the sounds (and smells) of tractors spreading slurry to fertilise and nourish the grass back to life after the cold months. Peter always laughed when his friends held their noses as the pungent odour drifted across the schoolyard. He laughed even harder when he told them it was cow's poo they were smelling!

Of all the machines on the farm, Peter liked tractors the best. He still remembered the day Dad arrived home in their new, shiny-green John Deere.

'Fear the Deere!' he thundered. Peter knew all the different types of tractors, but the John Deere was his favourite.

'If she's red …' started Mam.

'… leave her in the shed!' finished Peter.

'If she's blue ...' said Kate.

'... then she just won't do!' said Peter.

'If she's green ...' Dad continued.

'... you're fit to be seen!' chorused Mam and Kate and Peter together, laughing.

COCKADOOODLE DOOOOOO000000oooooooo!

A loud crow brought Peter back from his daydreaming. Was Rodney the Rooster getting up a bit late too? Blue whimpered.

'I know, girl,' smiled Peter. 'Time to get a move on.'

Chapter Two

The Bestest Eggs

Rodney the rooster belonged to Maggie and Eamon Cooper, who lived next door to Hazel Tree Farm, in Cooper's Cottage. They were older than Peter and Kate's parents, although the children weren't quite sure how much older, and no one, it seemed, wanted to tell them. Grownups were always a bit weird about telling people their ages. At her last birthday, Kate couldn't *wait* to blow out the giant '8'-shaped candle on her cake. Being eight was far more grown up than being seven. And when Peter turned ten, his cake was nearly ablaze with all the candles – it felt brilliant!

Maggie and Eamon had children of their own, but they were adults now and living away from Cooper's Farm. Their older child, Tom, was in Australia.

'Tom has just started a new job in a counting,' Kate had explained to Mam, after she heard the news from Maggie. 'He says it's hard work.'

'What's so hard about counting all day long?' Peter wondered.

'I dunno. I would be amazing at it,' said Kate.

Maggie and Eamon also had a daughter, Bernadette, who was in university in Cork. Peter had vague memories of Bernadette minding him and baby Kate. Now she was studying to be a dentist, and the children were hoping she didn't need anyone to practise on!

Eamon Cooper worked with Dad on the farm. In fact, for as long as anyone could remember, there had always been a Cooper working at Hazel Tree Farm. It was a tradition going back as far as Eamon's great-grandfather. It was Eamon's grandfather who built the large stone wall that ran all the way around the farmyard. Eamon loved to show the children the stone he had put in place when he was just nine years old. (It was easy to spot as it was more crooked than all the rest.)

'I was so chuffed to be allowed put that stone in,' he'd say, with a smile. 'My mother even made me a packed lunch, just like my dad and grandad's: a hard-boiled egg, cheese sandwiches, and buttermilk in an old jam jar.'

Peter and Kate would wince when they heard about food from the 'olden days'. No juice, crisps or chicken wraps!

'What's buttermilk?' Peter dared to ask one time, with a scrunched-up face.

'Back then, we made our own butter,' Eamon explained. 'We put milk into a big barrel called a butter churn and turned it up and over. We would do that again and again until we could hear something clunking around the inside of the barrel.'

'What was it?' asked Kate, her eyes wide. 'What was making the noise?'

'Butter!' laughed Eamon. 'A ball of beautiful, fresh butter hitting off the inside of the churn. And any milk left over was ours to drink, or my mother would use it to make brown bread.'

'Totally gross,' said Peter, shaking his head.

'Totally,' agreed Kate.

As well as Eamon's work at Hazel Tree, he helped Maggie run a small poultry farm, where they kept hens and a (very noisy) rooster called Rodney. Maggie grew up on a farm too, but on the other side of the world – she was from the Caribbean island of Trinidad. Her parents kept cows and goats, while Maggie was in charge of the hens. When she was a young woman, she came to Ireland to study agriculture, met Eamon, fell in love, and never left. She used to tell the children that people are different the world over, but chickens are the same!

Nowadays, Cooper's Farm Eggs were on the shelves of

every corner shop and supermarket in the area. Their eggs were so famous that chefs off the telly even used them in their cooking and baking. Maggie had a collection of signed photographs along her kitchen wall; Freddy Flynn from *The Bestest Bake Off* was her favourite.

'He said my eggs were by far the tastiest, and he would use no others,' Maggie boasted constantly.

COCKADOOODLE DOOOOOO00000oooooooo!

Rodney was still crowing as Peter made his way down the stairs, with Blue trotting behind.

'Well, good morning, sleepyhead!' laughed Mam, pouring cereal into her bowl. 'What time do you call this?'

'It's nearly eight o'clock,' Kate said disapprovingly as she carefully buttered her toast. She liked to make sure all the corners were covered in butter and none of it ran over the edges, creating a buttery mess.

Suddenly Peter had a wickedly brilliant idea. 'What's that?' he asked, pointing behind his sister.

Kate turned and Peter snatched the perfectly buttered toast. Just like Blue and her morning wakeup call, he licked the slice from top to bottom. Kate turned back, catching her brother mid-lick.

'Mam!' she roared. 'Peter's being disgusting!'

'Stop it, the pair of you,' said Mam, swapping the plates and giving Kate two new non-licked slices. 'Stop being disgusting,

Peter,' she added, trying to stop the corners of her mouth from curling upwards in a smile.

Mam secretly found Peter's pranks funny, and even though they did cause her children to squabble, it never lasted long. In fact, the two of them were as thick as thieves and the best of friends.

Thinking no one was appreciating his joke, Peter huffily nibbled on his toast. So what if he was up late – it was Friday, after all, which was nearly Saturday.

COCKADOOODLE DOOOOOOooooooooooooo!

What was Rodney at?

'I thought roosters were supposed to do their cockadoodles at dawn,' said Mam.

'It's called crowing,' said Kate, matter-of-factly, 'and they can do it anytime, really.'

Peter rolled his eyes. 'Know-it-all,' he mumbled under his breath.

Ignoring her brother, Kate continued. 'They also crow to show who's the boss, or to keep the hens together and safe when there is a threat.'

PECK, PECK, PECK!

That sound at the back door could mean only one thing.

'Hettie!' cried Kate, jumping up happily. Blue, too, wagged her tail on hearing the pecks of her little pal.

Sure enough, it was Hettie, the little cream and brown

speckled hen, looking for a cheeky breakfast treat. Maggie had given Hettie to Kate when she was just a chick, and now they were inseparable. You could often find them hanging out in the garden or snoozing in the sun together.

Dad had helped Kate set up a corner of the bike shed especially for Hettie. It was close to the main house, and since Mam refused to let a hen live in the kitchen, it had been a pretty good compromise. There was a straw box, a roost to sit on, a drinker for water and a bowl to put her grain in. Everything a little hen could want! Dad cut a hen-sized hole in a large sheet of wood and placed it in the doorway so Hettie could go in and out as she pleased.

At night, the main door of the shed was closed over to make sure Hettie was kept safely in and predators out. Then every morning, on his way to the farm, Dad opened it up and laughed as Hettie ran out and headed straight for the back door of the farmhouse.

Now Kate was throwing some crumbs and crusts to her little friend, smiling as the little hen picked and pecked and swallowed them down.

Kate loved animals – she wanted to be a vet like her mam when she was older. And it seemed she was already starting on her career path. All too often, Mam opened the hot press to see an array of wildlife recovering in 'Kate's Hospital'.

'KATE!' Mam would call out. 'It's time the baby birds left.

They have done their poos all over the pillowcases!'

Kate didn't just care about birds. Wild cats weren't wild for too long once Kate started feeding them (and their kittens). Rabbits and squirrels too. She had tried to sneak in a nest of mice once, but Mam caught her at the door and made her bring them back to the farmyard and then take a bath with loads of soap. Rodents were banned after that.

This March morning at the breakfast table, Kate's nose was buried in one of her favourite books: *1,000 Absolutely Amazing Animal Facts*.

'Did you know a group of crows is called a "murder" of crows, and a herd of elephants is also known as a "memory" of elephants?' she shouted randomly, at no one in particular. 'Isn't that funny? A memory of elephants. Everyone knows that an elephant never forgets.'

'Oh yeah, that's hilarious,' said Peter, sarcastically.

'And,' said Kate, staring her brother down, 'the girl elephants are the bosses.'

'Where's Dad?' asked Peter, suddenly noticing that his dad's breakfast bowl was untouched at the end of the table.

'Your poor dad has been up all night in the lambing shed,' said Mam. 'We have a set of twins and another set of triplets.'

'Five new lambs!' grinned Peter. 'Amazing, the fields will be full of lambs soon.'

But Kate looked worried. Twins were the norm for most

sheep. Ewes had two teats and could easily feed two babies, but anything more and sometimes they struggled to feed and supply enough milk for all of them.

'Are the lambs ok?' she asked.

But before Mam could answer, a voice called out from the door, 'Nearly all of them.'

A weary-looking Dad was home from a long night. Cradled in his arms was a tiny lamb. 'This poor fella has been rejected,' he said glumly. 'He's one of three and came right at the end. His poor mum was too exhausted dealing with the other two.'

'He doesn't look big enough or strong enough to fight for his feed,' sighed Mam, heading over to Dad.

Kate gasped, a lump rising in her throat. 'Is he … dead?' she whispered.

'No,' said Dad. 'He's a brave little one. I managed to get some milk into him, but it wasn't enough. He needs our help.'

Mam went to get a feeding tube. 'He will need to be stomach-tubed,' she said. 'We'll put the milk directly into his tummy.'

In the fridge were little bottles of colostrum, also known as 'first milk', which Dad had taken from other ewes who had just given birth and had it to spare. He had stored it in the fridge in preparation for a situation just like this. Colostrum had all the nutrition these new arrivals needed to be fit and healthy, so it was really important that this little lamb got his fair share.

Placing the weak little creature in the basket beside the stove, Dad gently raised his head as Mam passed a tube into his mouth, down his tiny throat and into his tummy. Once the tube was in place, Mam took the syringe full of magical, creamy colostrum and squeezed the fluid down the tube. She did it very slowly so as not to harm the lamb.

'Come on, little one, just try it,' coaxed Mam.

The lamb tossed his head, then began to slowly drink the milk through the tube.

'He's taking it,' said Peter under his breath, afraid he might put everyone off.

The children watched their parents work together, Dad gently holding the little lamb's head as Mam slowly pushed down on the syringe so more of its contents went down the tube.

'Look at him go,' whispered Kate in delight.

'We'll need to do this regularly for the next twenty-four hours, including overnight,' said Dad. 'Any takers on doing the night feeds?'

'Me, me!' cried the children together, shooting up their hands.

'Hold on there, you two. You can help by finishing your own breakfasts,' said Mam, not taking her eyes off the little lamb. 'The bus will be here soon. It's time for school.'

Grabbing their bags, Peter and Kate headed for the gate to

wait for the bus, already wishing the day away so they could get home to check on the lamb.

'Have a great day!' called Mam as she watched the last of the colostrum go down the tube.

'We will,' cried the children in unison as they slammed the door behind them.

The sound of the slamming door startled the trespasser. She had been watching the goings on at Hazel Tree Farm for a few days now. She followed the scent of lamb all the way to the house, but now it was mingled with so many other smells ... hen ... humans ... and (her ears pricked and twitched in annoyance) ... dog.

She watched as the small humans climbed up the steps of the school bus. As it pulled away, she lifted her head once again, her nostrils searching for the scent of lamb one last time. But it was gone, protected by the others, safe ... for now, perhaps.

Turning away from the house, she fled, back to the bushes, back to the wood, back to hiding.

Her mission was over for today. She would have to wait for another chance to call again.

Chapter Three

An Unwelcome

Visitor

Rat Tic Tic, Rat Tic Tic, Rat Tic Tic, Rat Tic Tic, Rat Tic Tic, Rat Tic Tic

On this particular morning, it wasn't Blue who woke Peter up – it was his bedroom window.

Hazel Tree farmhouse was very old, and not everything worked so well. The water pipes thumped into action when the heating was put on. The floorboards creaked (sometimes for no reason whatsoever), and the windows rattled every time the smallest gust of air found its way between the glass and the wooden panels.

'You'll soon get used to it,' Dad had told him when Peter

complained. 'I did when I slept there. In fact, I would make up songs and rhymes in time with the rattles.'

Dad stared out the window as if lost in thought. Then he tapped his chin and his eyes lit up. Peter and Kate looked at each other in horror – was their father about to recite a poem?

Rat a tat tat,
Can you hear that?
Rat a tee tee,
Sways the old tree ...

At this point, Dad stood up and swayed back and forth, arms in the air.

Rat a tic tic,
Could it be a stick?
Rat a til til,
On the windowsill ...

As he finished, Dad turned to his family in anticipation of their appreciation.

'Don't give up the day job,' said Kate.

'I think I prefer the rattles,' added Peter.

'Hey!' cried Dad, trying to sound offended.

Tic Tic, Rat Tic Tic, Rat Tic Tic, Rat Tic Tic, Rat Tic Tic, Rat Tic Tic, Rat

The rattles seemed extra bad this morning. Peter pulled the sides of his pillow to try and cover his ears. The noise was muffled, and Peter felt a wave of lovely, dreamy sleep cover over him. He was just about to doze back off, when …

COCKADOOODLE DOOOOOO000000ooooooo

COCKADOOODLE DOOOOOO000000ooooooo!

It was Rodney the rooster's turn now!

'Arrrrggghhhh,' Peter moaned. These animals and this house never wanted him to sleep again.

Blinking and rubbing his sleepy eyes, Peter instinctively moved his hand down by his bedside, waiting for it to fall on Blue's soft black fur.

'Wake up, sleepyhead,' he said with a grin. 'It's Saturday, and you know what that means!'

Saturdays at Whitehorn were a big event for Peter and Blue, and something was telling Peter that today was going to be extra special.

* * *

Every Saturday for the past few months, Eamon had taken Peter and Blue out for sheepdog training. And not just any training – Eamon had high hopes that Blue could be a champion at sheep trials.

Blue was a border collie, a breed known for their instincts, speed and intelligence, and Eamon had given her to Peter when she was just a pup. Peter named her Blue because of her unusual eyes: one brown and one blue.

'Now I can teach you how to be a real herdsman,' Eamon had said to a beaming Peter, as he took the wriggly little ball of fur in his arms. Blue's mother Peg was a champion, so Blue had big paws to fill.

'Did you know border collies can run up to 45km per hour?' piped up Kate, much to everyone's amusement – except for Peter, who just rolled his eyes.

From the moment they met, Peter and Blue had clicked and went everywhere together. As a pup, Blue loved to go into the fields to watch Eamon and Peg at work. Her mother was truly skilled in the art of herding sheep, and she and Eamon were a perfect match. Sometimes Blue would try to help but only ended up getting in the way.

'There's plenty of time for you to learn, little one,' a laughing Eamon would say as he carried her back to Peter. 'Best to sit back and watch for now.'

But the universe had other plans. One day, Peg suddenly became sick, very sick, and despite Mam's best efforts, she couldn't be saved.

'She's very unwell,' Mam had explained. 'I'm sorry, Eamon, but there's nothing we can do for her.'

'Is she in pain?' Eamon had asked.

'I'm afraid so,' said Mam. 'The kindest thing would be to

put her to sleep so she doesn't suffer any more.'

Eamon was devastated. He buried Peg in the corner of the top field, where she had spent so many happy days herding and rounding up sheep. Eamon remembered how her ears would stand straight up on the sound of his whistle calling her back.

Even months on, whenever Peg's name came up, Eamon, with a heavy heart, would remember 'the best dog I ever had'.

Now that Blue was a bit older and no longer a clumsy, cheeky pup, Eamon began training her and Peter to be champions too. Whatever the weather, he never let them miss a Saturday session.

But lately, things had not been going to plan, and Eamon was beginning to wonder if the talent in the family had ended with Peg's passing. Despite his best efforts, he couldn't seem to get this young dog to respond to the most basic of commands, and he was becoming more and more frustrated.

Dad kept a small flock of sheep aside for them to practise with, and today, Peter and Blue were facing a dress rehearsal of a real sheepdog trial. It was going to be a challenge to see how good Blue could be.

As Peter reached down to pat Blue on the morning of the big test, she was not in her usual place beside his bed. He sat bolt upright.

'Blue!' he called out. 'Blue, where are you?'

But his dog was nowhere to be seen. And why was the house so quiet?

'Larry!' Peter suddenly exclaimed, remembering the little lamb downstairs. The children had named him Larry after their favourite uncle, who lived in America (and whose hair always looked a bit woolly!).

Peter jumped out of bed and quickly got dressed. He was still pulling his hoodie over his head as he tumbled through the kitchen door.

'Shhhhhhhhh' – Mam placed her fingers to her lips – 'you'll wake them.'

Lying in his basket in front of the stove, Larry was fast asleep. His little belly, rounded and full after a night of bottle feeds, rose up and down on each breath. And sure enough, there was Blue, curled up beside him, her sheepdog instincts telling her that this little lamb needed extra protection. She glanced up at Peter, her tail wagging gently before her eyes closed once more and she continued to doze.

'That's the girl,' Peter whispered, smiling.

Blue wasn't the only one tired after the night before. Kate, wrapped in a blanket, lay sleeping on a chair in the corner. She had been up all night with Mam, afraid to leave Larry's side.

Peter gently crouched down beside Larry and touched his soft fleece. 'Will he be ok, Mam?' he asked.

A smile spread across his mother's exhausted face. 'I think

so,' she said. 'He drank everything I gave him. I think he's over the worst.'

'What happens now?' asked Peter.

'Hopefully another of the ewes will adopt him,' said Mam, touching Peter's shoulder.

'Hopefully?' echoed Peter, not convinced by his mother's answer. 'But what if they don't? What will happen to him?'

'Don't worry,' Mam said, smiling. 'I am sure we will find a new mum for Larry.'

Somewhat reassured, Peter sat down to his breakfast. He didn't notice how Mam's smile had faded. As she watched the sleeping lamb, Mam knew only too well how little time was left if they were to have a successful adoption.

In a perfect world, Larry would have been fostered out straight away to a ewe who had just given birth; a ewe who was an experienced mother, with only one lamb of her own. That way, her own lamb and her adopted lamb would both have enough milk in those early days. But this had not been possible, and now, as time passed, there was an ever-growing chance that Larry would be rejected. He needed so much more than a warm stove and syringes of colostrum if he was going to make it.

Where there is livestock, there is dead stock, Mam thought to herself. That was what her father used to say whenever an animal died on their farm.

She remembered a night long ago when she and her father

were helping one of their heifers to calve. It was her first birth, and she was in a lot of difficulty and struggling to deliver. Mam and her father worked tirelessly through the night, but to no avail.

'Run to the house and call the vet,' her father cried when things got really bad. By the time Mam returned, the calf was delivered, but it only lived for a few minutes. Its mother, exhausted, lay beside it.

Mam's father stood outside the stall, cap in hand and head lowered. She could still picture his face as he turned towards her, smiling kindly as he wiped the tears that ran down her face. 'We did our best,' he said gently. 'Where there is livestock, there is dead stock.'

It was in one of those moments that Mam had decided to become a vet. She wanted to do everything she could to give animals a chance at life. To always do her best, just like her dad did.

Now as she looked at Peter and Kate bonding with Larry, she knew it may soon be her turn to comfort her own children. If things didn't work out as they hoped, little hearts could be broken.

The harshness of February was a distant memory, as the snowdrops gave way to those daffodils brave enough to bloom in the still-chilly air. 'March comes in like a lion and out like a lamb,' Mam used to say about her favourite month, which brought the promise of summer and warmer days to pass.

Out in the fields, Dad too was noticing a change in the seasons. It had been a bleak winter, but now spring was definitely in the air. He watched his growing flock of sheep graze happily in the fields. It was a perfect day for these new mums to be outside, with the sun on their backs. Some of the braver lambs were running about and playing together, while others, feeling a little timid, stayed close to their mothers.

Dad was still worried about Larry. Like Marian, he understood only too well that time was not on their side. She and Kate had worked wonders with their night feeds, and Larry was certainly over the worst. Now the next stage was up to him. He had a ewe who might just turn out to be the perfect foster mother, but he wouldn't say anything to the children yet. He didn't want to raise their hopes in case it didn't work out. That's the problem with farming and livestock: things don't always go to plan.

Through the kitchen window, Peter could hear the happy bleats of the sheep in the fields and the clucking of hens coming from Cooper's Farm. One cluck seemed to be louder and closer than all the others. The familiar *PECK, PECK, PECK!* at the back door told them that Hettie the hen was here for her morning visit.

'Hettie,' Kate murmured dreamily from her chair in the corner, her eyes still closed. She stretched and rubbed her eyes open, then headed over to the back door.

The little hen trotted in, awaiting her breakfast and a cuddle with Kate. Her arrival stirred Blue, who yawned and stretched and let out a morning yelp. This was soon followed by Larry, who also woke up and realised he was feeling a little peckish.

Mmmmaaaaaaaaa! came his little bleat, which made the children giggle.

'Morning, Larry,' mumbled Kate, who was now munching on some toast. Crumbs sprayed from her mouth and Hettie hopped off her lap and pecked around her feet.

Cluck Cluck Cluck, went the hen.

Whine, gruff, gruff, whine, went the dog.

Maaaa maaaa maaaa, went the lamb.

'All right, that's it.' Mam had had enough. She had been up all night, and her kitchen was turning into a zoo. 'Out you two go and bring your animal friends with you. Larry is due his next feed, and from the sounds of it, he wants it now.'

Leaving Mam and a very 'hangry' Larry behind, the children went outside with Blue and Hettie. The dog and the hen were firm friends, and it wasn't unusual to see a lazy Hettie hitch a ride on Blue's back every now and again. It was nearly time for Blue's training lesson, so they all headed straight over to the Coopers'.

Visits to Cooper's Farm were now part of the Saturday-morning routine. The kids would watch Blue having her lesson, followed by the most epic of experiences: Maggie's Treat Tin!

Maggie was the best baker the children had ever met. There was nothing she couldn't do with flour, sugar and eggs. She always made the cakes for the children's birthday parties. Cakes in the shape of Spider-Man, with a web made from sugar thread. Cakes in the shape of tractors, with liquorice wheels, or angels sitting on candy-floss clouds. Their favourite had been a volcano cake, which exploded orange chocolate lava after Peter blew out the candles. Maggie loved the taste of coconut and pineapple, which she said reminded her of childhood, and made the most delicious homemade ice creams in summertime.

'I hope she has more of those caramel squares,' said Peter as they made their way over. Peter's favourite thing (after Blue and tractors) was eating.

'Or those fairy cakes with the popping candy,' said Kate. 'They are so light and fluffy and fizzy; I feel like I can fly with just one bite.' She scooped up Hettie and did a little twirl.

'You're so weird,' sighed Peter.

Cooper's Farm was right next door to Hazel Tree. A long hedgerow, planted by the children's great-grandfather, was all that separated the two households. Even though there was a perfectly fine driveway into each house, everyone took the shortcut through the hedge instead. Over time, the hedge had given up trying to re-grow and cover up the gap, so its green leaves now formed a perfect arch for all who passed under it.

Walking through this small leafy portal, the children came to the Coopers' yard. The henhouse could be seen just over the boundary hedge, and if the wind blew a certain way, there was always the pungent smell of chicken poop.

'Awww, chicken slurry,' Mam would groan as she went to take in the washing from the line. 'Nothing clings to clothes like the stink of chicken slurry.'

Beyond the chicken yard, the children passed through the main gate and walked up the path to Cooper's Cottage. The cottage sat amongst beautiful rose bushes, which had been there for as long as anyone could remember.

'Only Coopers have ever lived at Cooper's Cottage,' Eamon liked to say proudly.

BANG THUMP BANG THUMP BANG THUMP BANG THUMP! Something or someone was making an awful lot of noise at the front of the house.

The kids saw Eamon nailing a sign to the fence. Maggie was dragging a large box to the front, which was full of eggs.

'Peter, Kate, you are just in time,' she said, panting from all the box-pulling. 'Don't just stand there – give me a hand. Push, push!'

The children ran and helped push the box into position.

'What's all this for?' asked Peter.

'Well, take a look here and see,' said Eamon, standing back to admire his work.

Peter looked up at the sign and read aloud, 'Fresh Free-Range Eggs, €2.50 per box.'

Nailed beside the sign was a wooden box with a small slit on the lid. It was just big enough for coins or folded notes.

'People can stop and buy eggs when passing by,' said Maggie, smiling.

'Will you be standing out here all day?' asked Peter.

'I certainly will not,' said Maggie. 'It's an honesty box.' Seeing the looks of confusion on the children's faces, she continued, 'People pick up the eggs and put the money in the box.'

'But what if they steal them?' asked Kate.

'Well, that's why we call it an honesty box,' said Eamon. 'We are relying on people's honesty and better nature to do the right thing.'

'Sounds risky to me,' said Peter, shaking his head.

'All right,' said Eamon, with a laugh. 'It's time to put Miss Blue here through her paces.'

Blue, hearing her name, did a little yelp and jump with excitement.

'I might just stay here and keep an eye on this honesty box thingy,' said Kate, still not convinced of the good nature of others.

'You are not staying here on your own, my darling,' said Maggie, putting her arm around Kate. 'Come on, you can help me find more eggs. We'll check back on the box in a little while.'

As the happy troupe headed down the lane and into the yard, they saw some of the hens out scratching and throwing up dust. Hettie ran towards them to join in the fun. Rodney the rooster was fussing around, flapping and trotting from group to group.

'Goodness me, what a fuss that boy is making,' said Eamon. 'Has himself all in a tizzy the past couple of days.'

'Something is bothering him,' said Maggie, frowning. 'Our Rodney is really minding his girls lately.'

'What do you mean?' asked Kate.

'Well, I think a few of the hens are clucking,' said Maggie, 'which means they are broody and ready to hatch some chicks. I've put eggs under them in their nesting boxes.'

'How do you know which are chicks and which are regular eggs?' asked Peter.

'Well,' said Maggie, 'the hens will sit on the eggs, and this creates enough warmth to help the chicks develop.'

'It's called incubation,' piped up Kate, proudly.

'Will the chicks be here this week?' asked Peter, excited now.

'No,' said Maggie. 'It'll be about three weeks before we see any little fluffballs on the farm. The hens will sit on the eggs for all that time.'

'Hang on,' said Peter. 'I had a boiled egg this morning. Could that have been a chick?'

'Did you not listen before you cracked the shell?' Eamon exclaimed, winking at Maggie.

Peter's face fell in horror.

Maggie threw up her hands, motioning for Eamon to be quiet. 'Stop teasing the children, Eamon! No, Peter, the eggs you have for your breakfast have not been sat on by the mama hen, so there are no little chicks inside. Isn't that right, Eamon?'

She glared back at her husband, who was still chuckling to himself.

As they neared the henhouse, Blue stopped dead in her tracks.

Grrruufff! Her bark signalled that something was wrong.

Watching her and then looking into the distance, Eamon gave her a tug on her collar. 'Come on, girl,' he said, shaking his head. 'There's nothing out there.'

But something was out there, and it was watching them. Something that had been there before.

The trespasser had returned.

Crouching low, the young vixen found the perfect spot to see all that was going on. Lambs were now outdoors, ready for the taking. Or maybe a nice plump hen (or two) would be on the dinner menu. One thing for sure, there was plenty of food here to feed her hungry cubs back in the den.

COCKADOOODLE DOOOOOO000000oooooo!

But that rooster could be a problem, and that dog too. They were alerting the humans to her presence. If she was to have a successful hunt, she would need to act fast and soon.

Letting out a low growl, the vixen slipped away. No one was any the wiser to the danger that awaited … No one, it seemed, except for Rodney and Blue.

Chapter Four

Treats & Trials

Eamon lifted the silver whistle to his mouth. A long, shrill tune rang out across the valley. 'Away to me! Away to me!' his voice boomed.

Blue's ears pricked up. At great speed, she veered right and towards the small, huddled herd of sheep, anticipating their next move.

'Lie down,' came Eamon's next command.

Blue fell to the ground, panting, her eyes fixed on him.

Peter looked on with joy. Blue was doing brilliantly. Eamon's commands were clear and stern, and his whistle was the perfect pitch.

Peter wanted a whistle of his own, but Eamon had insisted he learn how to whistle himself, just in case the day ever came when he needed to call Blue in an emergency.

'I've misplaced many a whistle over the years,' said Eamon, 'but you can't lose your own natural whistle once you've mastered it.'

At first, despite his best efforts, Peter just couldn't whistle. He'd try, but only spit would come out and a funny *prrrrrrph* sound. But with practice, he was getting better. And now, as he watched Blue in action, he saw that she was getting better with practice too. The past few months of hard work were really paying off.

'She's coming on well, young Peter,' Eamon said, sounding proud. 'Maybe we will make a champion out of this dog yet.'

Peter thought he would burst with pride.

Then suddenly, three brave ewes broke from the herd and took off towards the far hedge. Blue was quick to her feet and ready for action.

'Come bye, come bye!' Eamon's command told Blue to move left.

Blue ran wide, drawing in on the sheep and gathering them into the corner of the hedge. She crouched low, fixing her stare on the strays.

Eamon watched, waiting to see what she would do next. Peter knew this was the deciding moment: did Blue have what it takes to be a champion like her mum?

To reunite the strays with the rest of the herd, Blue would have to position herself between the sheep and the hedge, pushing the strays out of their holding area and running them back to the rest of the group. For a young dog, this was a daunting task. Moving between the hedge and herd could leave her open to injury. The sheep might kick or attack what they believed was a predator and Blue would be trapped.

Blue crouched low and moved stealthily, then paused.

'Steady, steeeeeaaaady …' Eamon's tone was calm and cautious.

For the smallest moment, Peter felt as if the world stood still. The birds grew quiet in the trees, and even the wind died down in preparation for what was to come next. The only sound he could hear was his heart beating inside his chest.

'That's it, Blue,' he whispered under his breath. 'That's it, girl.'

But the calmness was not to last. Blue, overexcited and inexperienced, burst forward and ran straight for the stray sheep, scattering them in all directions.

Eamon ran forward to try and block their escape.

'Away to me, away to me!' he called to Blue, asking her to move clockwise and try to regroup the animals before more damage was done.

The strays were now heading back to the main herd, so maybe all was not lost. But when one sheep lagged behind,

Blue forgot her training and reverted to her predatory instincts. She jumped towards the animal, biting at its neck to bring it down.

This was the final straw for Eamon. 'LIE DOWN!' he boomed. He was really cross now. Nipping or biting a sheep would cause a dog to be disqualified from a sheep trial. Blue knew better than this.

Blue immediately dropped to the ground, realising she was in trouble. The sheep, now free, ran towards the rest of the herd, frightened from her ordeal.

Eamon shook his head, taking off his cap and scratching his forehead. 'I don't know,' he said wearily. 'I just don't know.'

He looked over at Blue, who lay on the ground, panting. 'You're nothing like your mother. Nothing like her at all. I'm sorry, Peter, but maybe Blue doesn't have what it takes.'

Blue didn't like how her humans looked. Eamon's face was sad, and Peter's head was lowered. She cautiously wagged her tail, hoping this might lighten the mood.

Peter was so disappointed. He was sure Blue could be a top sheepdog, and he wanted nothing more than to hold a trophy aloft as a champion herder, like Eamon had been with Peg.

Figuring she was in trouble, Blue let out a small whine and rested her head on her paws. Peter walked towards her, as her tail continued to slowly wag back and forth. She hoped for some kind words and affection from her favourite human.

'You'll have to tell your father it's no use, she just doesn't have it in her,' mumbled Eamon, placing his whistle into his pocket and his cap back on his head. 'Away off with you. We're done for the day.'

The lesson was over. Eamon, on his own, brought the sheep back to the main yard.

Peter and Blue followed behind. Blue kept close to her young master's side, watching him and waiting for a smile in her direction, an indication that all was well once again. She didn't have to wait long. With Eamon out of sight, Peter reached down and patted her head with the gentle nature she adored.

'It's ok, girl,' he whispered. 'We'll get it right. All we need is more practice.'

Woof! a delighted Blue agreed.

'I found another one!' roared Kate.

The hens had taken to laying eggs wherever they wanted, and Kate and Maggie were hunting high and low. Behind sheds, in bushes, under trees – it was tiring work, but egg-hunting was also fun.

Kate took a break and headed back to the main gate to check how the honesty box was doing.

'Maggie!' she shouted in alarm. 'Maggie, come quick!'

Thinking there was trouble, Maggie hurried over, her basket of eggs swinging with each stride.

'What is it, child?' she gasped. 'Did you hurt yourself?'

'No,' sobbed Kate, 'it's the eggs. They're all gone. They've all been stolen. Peter was right, this was a bad idea.'

Putting her hand into her cardigan pocket, Maggie fished out a little key. She placed it into the keyhole of the wooden box and turned it gently.

'Stolen, eh?' she said, with a smile. 'Nope! In fact, I do believe we have sold out.'

'What!' exclaimed Kate, standing on her tippy toes to see for herself.

Inside the little box was the most money Kate had ever seen.

'I don't believe it!' she squealed. 'Quick, Maggie, we have to stock up. We don't want to disappoint our honest customers!'

Maggie let out a huge laugh. 'We've done enough business for today, my little one.' She handed another sign to Kate. 'Hang this up for me, if you please.'

Kate read aloud: 'Sold out. Come back tomorrow.' She beamed. Maggie had thought of everything!

She hung it over the box, still hardly able to believe it had worked.

Hmmmm, she thought to herself, *what else can we sell?*

She heard Eamon, Peter and Blue coming back to the

house. It was finally time for something tasty from Maggie's Treat Tin!

* * *

With great anticipation, the children stood behind Maggie as she reached into the press and took out the precious tin. She opened the lid and presented the contents to them as if they were the crown jewels. And to Peter and Kate, they actually were! Blueberry muffins, fairy cakes, choc chip cookies … Maggie's treat tin was the best.

'Caramel squares!' the children squealed in unison. Eamon laughed as he put on the kettle, secretly planning to steal a treat (or two) for himself.

'Yes,' said Maggie, 'and made with real chocolate. None of that cooking chocolate nonsense round here.' She stuck out her tongue in disgust at the thought.

The children's hands dived in.

'They're the best,' said Peter, spraying shortbread crumbs everywhere as he spoke.

'Say it, don't spray it,' said Kate, doing her best karate moves to avoid the flying crumbs.

A piece of paper stuck to the fridge caught Peter's eye as he chomped. He moved forward to get a closer look. 'Ballynoe Autumn Fair,' he said, reading the flyer aloud.

'Ooh, a fair!' said Kate, her eyes aglow.

'Yes,' said Maggie. 'Isn't it wonderous news? There hasn't been a fair in Ballynoe for so many years. I am really looking forward to the cooking demonstrations. Freddy Flynn, the chef off the telly, is coming. Did I ever tell you what he said about our eggs?'

'Maybe once or twice,' muttered Eamon, a little sarcastically. The children giggled, but Maggie ignored her husband and carried on anyway.

'He praised my eggs for making his sponge cake the tastiest, his cookies the crunchiest, and his meringues the lightest.' Maggie looked away as if lost in a dream.

'Could me and Blue enter the sheepdog trials?' Peter asked Eamon.

'After today's shenanigans,' sighed Eamon, 'I don't think so. She'd make fools of us.'

'Eamon Cooper!' Maggie was snapped out of her daydream by her husband's sharp words. 'How can you say such a thing?'

'Blue is nothing like her mother,' Eamon replied. 'There isn't enough time in the world to get that dog ready.'

'Nonsense,' replied Maggie. 'There was once a time you thought the same about Peg.'

'I thought no such thing!' Eamon answered back, feeling a little cross now. His beloved Peg was a champion.

'Oh yes, you did.' Maggie wasn't giving in. 'She would hang

out of a sheep's tail and jump into the middle of flocks looking for them to play with her. All she needed was time – you used to say it yourself – and when her time came, she was truly the best. Maybe our Blue is like her mother, a late bloomer, and just needs that one chance to prove herself.'

Hmmmph. Eamon shrugged off his wife's words and walked over to the glass cabinet in the corner. He took a gold trophy down from the top shelf and blew the dust off it before showing it to the children.

'This was the first trophy I won with Peg,' said Eamon sadly. 'It wasn't the biggest competition in the world, but that was the day I knew my Peg was very special. I don't think there will ever be a dog like her again. Blue is nothing like her.'

Hearing her name, Blue wagged her tail.

'Peg was the best dog I ever had,' Eamon said again, placing the trophy back in its cabinet.

Not wanting to hurt her feelings, he gave Blue a pat on the head as he passed. 'But maybe you have another talent we just don't know about.'

'My, my, what a Negative Ninny,' said Maggie, when Eamon had left the room. She handed the children the treat tin for another round. 'Pay him no mind, you two. Young Blue will have her day, you'll see.'

'Do you really think Blue could be a champion, Maggie?' Peter asked, his voice sad. He was so disappointed and was trying to hide the tears that were close to falling.

'Yes, I do,' said Maggie, enveloping him in a massive hug. 'Now let's talk about this fair. What else will be there, do you think?'

Peter's face brightened. 'Ice cream!'

'Always thinking about food, Peter,' said Kate, rolling her eyes. 'Could I enter Hettie in the Best Pet competition?'

'I don't see why not,' said Maggie, adding Kate to the hug.

Finding his smile once again, Peter also found his appetite and reached for another caramel square.

'You should enter your cakes, Maggie,' Kate suggested. 'You'd win first prize.'

'I don't mind helping with the testing,' Peter said with a grin, chocolate and caramel smeared across his teeth.

'Peter!' Kate was disgusted. 'Don't speak with your mouth full!'

'Hmmmm, maybe I will enter,' said Maggie, not really paying attention.

'I bet Mrs Reilly is entering,' said Kate, scooping out the cream in her fairy cake.

'What makes you say that?' asked Maggie, suddenly interested.

'Her daughter, Karen, is in my class,' said Kate. 'I brought in some of my birthday cake for Teacher last year, the unicorn one that you made.'

'I remember,' said Maggie. 'Sugar white with a frothy pink sponge on the inside.'

'Well,' Kate continued, 'Teacher said it was by far the nicest, spongiest sponge he had ever tasted, when next thing Karen Reilly shouts up that her mother's sponge is the nicest, and that their hen eggs are the best. She even spun her head around and stuck her tongue out at me!'

'Oh, those Reillys!' Maggie erupted. 'They only have a few hens, and the last time I saw them, they looked as if their egg-laying days were well and truly behind them. In fact, I saw Karen's mother, Monica Reilly, with my own two eyeballs buying our eggs in the shop.'

The children giggled. Sometimes Maggie's phrases weren't quite right.

'You mean, your own two *eyes*,' laughed Kate.

'I know what I mean,' smirked Maggie, as she dusted the cookie crumbs from her hands. She strode with purpose to her bookshelf, grabbing her recipe book from the top shelf.

'I think it's time I showed that Monica Reilly who is top baker round here,' she said firmly, leafing through the well-thumbed pages.

'What are you planning, Maggie Cooper?' Eamon had returned and was reaching into the tin of goodies next to his wife.

'Never you mind, Mr Eamon Cooper!' Maggie said, snapping the lid shut and nearly catching Eamon's fingers as she did so. 'But you can be sure I will be baking up a storm in this cottage. I have a score to settle with Monica Reilly once and for all.'

'Oh, not this again,' Eamon groaned. His wife's quarrel with Monica Reilly had gone on long enough. 'Does it really matter whose eggs or whose sponge is the best?' He peeled down the wrapper of the bun he managed to grab just in time.

Maggie glared at her husband. 'Whose side are you on, Eamon Cooper? Right, it's time I created the ultimate show-stopper.'

She sat at the kitchen table and put on her glasses, which hung from a chain around her neck: a sign that she meant business.

'Come on, you two,' Eamon said, beckoning the children. 'Let's leave Mrs Bakes-a-Lot to her plotting.'

Maggie gently lifted the lid of the tin and nodded to the children to take another treat.

Peter and Kate glanced at each other and snuck yet another bun out of the box before running out the door after Eamon.

'Eat those after your dinners!' Maggie roared after them. 'Or else your mother will be very cross with me!'

From the yard, the children waved goodbye to Eamon, who was nearly run over by Blue and Hettie as they hurried back to Hazel Tree too.

Chapter Five

Larry's (Little) Presents

aaaaaaa!

Peter and Kate heard the little bleat as soon as they got to the back door of Hazel Tree farmhouse.

'Larry!' Kate cried. 'You're awake!'

A lively Larry was waddling around the kitchen table. He was following Mam, who was doing her best not to step on him.

'Someone is starting to feel much better,' said Mam. 'Grab that bottle, Kate. I think it's time you two took over Larry duties.'

Seeing the bottle in Kate's hand, Larry turned sharply, slipping on the kitchen floor as he tried to get to her as fast as possible. Kate bent down and scooped him up. Settling back into the large armchair, she held the bottle and watched with glee as the little lamb gripped tightly onto its teat.

Suck suck suck! To Kate, it was the most adorable sound ever.

Larry's tail was wagging, and his little tummy got rounder with each mouthful. It wasn't long until he was finished. He nudged the empty bottle, looking for more.

'That's enough for now, little man,' said Kate, scratching his head. Realising there was no more milk (for now), Larry curled and nestled into Kate's lap. He rested his head and began to snooze.

* * *

By that evening, Larry had really turned a corner and was proving to be an inquisitive little lamb. The children played with him and fed him. They showed him all around the house, and he snuggled in Kate's arms as she snuck him up the stairs.

'No lambs upstairs!' Mam called out, but her demands fell on deaf ears. Larry was already snooping around bathrooms and bedrooms, walking into wardrobes and leaving little presents as he went.

'Yuck!' said Peter. 'He's done a poo in the hall!'

'And one in my bedroom!' wailed Kate.

'What's this puddle?' asked Peter in disgust.

After cleaning up and putting Larry back in his basket for another nap, the children helped get dinner ready.

'So,' said Mam, as they sat down to enjoy sausage and mash,

'what are we all going to do for the Ballynoe Autumn Fair?'

'I've promised them some sheep for the sheepdog trials,' said Dad.

'I really want to enter Blue in the trials, but Eamon doesn't think she's ready,' said Peter glumly.

'Give her time, Peter,' said Dad, who had heard all about Blue's disastrous trial earlier that day. 'Sometimes the best flowers bloom last.'

'Well, I'm entering Hettie in the Best Pet competition,' said Kate, chomping on her sausage. 'She'll win for sure, or maybe Larry. He'd be so cute with a red ribbon.'

'Sweetheart, that might not be possible,' said Mam, glancing over at Dad.

'He'll be a fully grown ram by the time August comes,' said Peter, rolling his eyes.

'And we're hoping to get Larry fostered soon,' said Dad.

'Fostered?' asked Peter. 'So you found a ewe?'

Dad took a deep breath, realising that it was time to tell the children. 'I think so. Another ewe is due to deliver just one lamb any day now. It's not her first time, so she might have the instinct to take care of Larry too.'

Kate looked worried. 'But our scent is all over him. That could put a sheep off, couldn't it, Mam?'

'Yeah, your smell definitely would,' laughed Peter, holding his nose.

Kate kicked him under the table. 'Why can't we just keep him?' she begged.

'We have a whole field of Larrys,' replied Mam, reaching over to hold Kate's hand.

'Yes, I think we have enough animals going on here,' agreed Dad. 'Anyway, Larry needs to be with his friends, to learn sheep ways so he can grow up into a fine ram.'

'We can't teach him those things,' added Mam. 'Tomorrow, Dad will move him back to the shed and we can see about finding him a mummy of his own.'

Kate had to agree that it would be better for Larry this way, but she would be sad to say goodbye to their little friend.

'Fine,' she grumbled, though she didn't feel fine at all.

Peter felt sad too, but he understood the ways of farming. And anyway, without Larry to take care of, he would have more time to work with Blue, not to mention something else that was close to his heart …

'I guess that means I can be chief tester for Maggie's cakes for the fair,' he said, thinking out loud. 'She has to win!'

'Don't tell me,' said Mam, 'she wants to beat Monica Reilly.'

The children laughed.

Baaaaaaaaaaa! chorused Larry from his basket.

Yelp! went Blue, looking for some dinner of her own.

They waited for the familiar cluck of Hettie. When it didn't come, Mam looked around.

'Where's Hettie, Kate?' she asked.

'She wanted to be outside,' Kate replied, 'so I let her out. She's been acting strange lately, maybe something to do with the spring air.'

* * *

Later that evening, while the children were getting ready for bed, Mam and Dad settled down on the couch, Mam watching her favourite program and Dad reading the farming paper.

'Fingers crossed that ewe will lamb tomorrow,' Dad said, distractedly. 'It could be our only chance.'

'She's a good mother, too,' said Mam. 'And he's such a lovely little lamb. Hopefully by this time tomorrow, he'll be with a family of his own.'

Suddenly, Dad stopped reading. 'What is it with Monica Reilly and Maggie? Why are they such enemies?'

'Well,' said Mam, pausing the telly, 'it all started with a sponge cake. Monica Reilly is convinced Maggie bought a sponge cake and passed it off as her own at the Great Ballynoe Bake Off a few years back. The prize was a cooking lesson with that famous chef, Freddy Flynn. Maggie won, and what's more, she gave Freddy Flynn two dozen Cooper's Farm Eggs as a gift.'

'That was nice of her,' said Dad, a little confused.

'Don't you see what Maggie was up to?' Mam smiled. 'She told Freddy Flynn that Cooper hens lay the best eggs, and that was why her sponge was the best. Freddy Flynn has been using Cooper's Farm Eggs ever since, and he even thanked Maggie on live telly, saying his cakes have never tasted so good! Cooper's Farm Eggs flew off the shelves after that.'

'And the Reillys blamed Maggie for them losing some of that egg business,' Dad realised.

'Eggs-actly,' said Mam, laughing at her own joke.

Dad thought for a moment. 'Did Maggie' – he paused – 'you know, buy the cake in the first place?'

Mam threw him a shocked expression. 'David Farrelly, how could you say such a thing? Of course she didn't! When Maggie arrived in Ireland all those years ago, she was very homesick. She was a world away from Trinidad, and the Coopers did everything they could to bring some of the Caribbean to Ballynoe. Mrs Cooper was a great baker herself and learnt the recipe for a traditional sponge cake from Trinidad. Eamon is convinced that the night Maggie had a slice of Mrs Cooper's Trini Sponge Cake is the night she fell in love with Cooper's Cottage. She has been making 'Trini-Irish Sponge Cake' ever since.'

'So that recipe is 100% unique,' realised Dad.

'Yes,' said Mam, 'and it's been around longer than Monica Reilly.'

'And every slice is a little slice of heaven,' Dad laughed, licking his lips.

By now, the evening had drawn in dark and chilly. Elsewhere in Ballynoe, people were settling in for the night and children were getting ready for bed. For so many, the working day was over; Eamon's day, however, was not quite done. He walked around the farm, checking the hens and making sure all was as it should be.

Cooper's Farm wasn't as big as it had once been. Twenty years ago, there would have been over two thousand hens scuttling about. They were housed at night to protect them from the cold (and any predators that might come calling). But as Eamon and Maggie got older and their children moved away, they decided to keep a smaller flock. Cooper's Farm Eggs were still well known, but they were no longer sold all over the country – instead, Eamon and Maggie stuck with local stores and farmers markets, which was more than enough work for them and their beloved brood.

Eamon carefully checked the hens that were sitting in their nesting boxes, preparing for their new arrivals. In the main henhouse, others were perched in a line, sleeping soundly; the rest were wandering in the open space below. They had plenty of water and plenty of grain. *This is what free range is all about,*

Eamon thought as he stood in the doorway.

'Now it's time I let you ladies have your rest,' he said aloud.

Cock, cock, cock! crowed Rodney, gently. He was weary from all his fussing earlier.

'Apologies,' said Eamon, laughing. 'Bedtime for you too, Mr Rodney.'

Taking one final look, Eamon closed over the door, checking the handle to be sure that his birds were safe for the night.

One little hen, however, was not locked up safe and sound and instead was out on a secret mission of her own. Hettie had strayed away from the safety of her shed at Hazel Tree and made her way through the gap in the hedge. She waited until Eamon was gone before scurrying to the back of the henhouse, running under the fence and disappearing into the night.

* * *

Back at Hazel Tree, Kate was in a peaceful slumber, unaware that her little hen was far from home and all alone.

Rat Tic Tic Rat Tic Tic Rat Tic Tic Rat Tic Rat

Down the hall in Peter's room, it was anything but peaceful. Peter was at war once again with his rattly bedroom window.

'That should do it,' he announced triumphantly as he placed an ice-lolly stick into the gap. 'I'd like to see you rattle now!'

Turning from the troublesome window, he hopped back

into bed. He wrapped himself up nice and tight in his duvet. *Finally, some peace and quiet*, he thought, yawning.

Rat Tic Tic Tic Rat Rat Tic Tic Tic Rat, Rat Tic Tic Tic Rat Rat Tic Tic Rat Rat

'Are you kidding me!' Peter's eyes popped open, and he sat upright, furious.

Not only had his genius plan not worked, the noise was actually louder! The lolly stick added an extra *Tic Rat*!

Well, there's only thing for it, thought Peter, throwing back his bedcovers. *I'm leaving that window open tonight. If I don't, I'll never sleep again.*

With the window open onto a calm night, a gentle breeze drifted past Peter and into the room, happy, it seemed, to be allowed inside. April was just around the corner, and the worst of the harsh March weather had passed. Peter took a deep breath, filling his lungs with the cool air. He stretched, yawned, and headed back to bed, careful not to step on the dozing Blue, who was curled up in her usual spot at his bedside.

''Night, girl,' Peter said, gently stroking her ear. Finally, a good night's sleep lay ahead.

Or did it?

The vixen waited until the perfect darkness had come. The kind of darkness that felt like the world had come to a complete stop. Everything was still, everywhere was calm. The time to strike.

Making sure her cubs were warm and safe in their den, she set off into this perfect darkness. She weaved her way along the edges of the field, staying under the trees. She must be careful not to get trapped in a ray of moonlight that would light her up and give the game away. She was an expert hunter, using her senses to detect any danger ... or dinner. She sniffed the air and pricked her ears, which twitched as they followed the sounds that only she could hear: bats flying overhead, moths fluttering in the moonlight, and night-time breezes gliding over the blades of grass. To a vixen on the hunt, these were the sounds that kept her company and kept her alert.

Her first stop was going to be the henhouse. It would be easier to snatch some hens than a lamb – she wouldn't have to worry about an overly protective mother. An angry ewe could be very dangerous and could cost her time and energy. And knowing she had some hens stashed away meant that a plump lamb would be an added bonus.

The henhouse was right next to the field fence, ideal for a snatch and dash. The humans' den was close by, but this would be to her advantage – if the hens made a fuss, it would not matter. Their squawking and racket would distract the humans, giving her time to make her second strike, in the meadow. By the time the humans realised what was going on, she would be long gone and her little ones would have enough food for many days.

The roof of the henhouse grew larger – she was nearly there.

Grrrrrrrrr …

She picked up various scents wafting along the breeze. Dog: that could be a problem. It was coming from the other, larger human den. She would have to keep her distance so as not to rouse suspicion from that canny canine.

Then there was that rooster. He had nearly ruined her plans with his carry-on earlier, alerting the dog and one of the humans. He'd better not get in her way, if he knew what was good for him.

The shed rooftops were silhouettes in the night sky. The faint glow from the farmhouses told her the humans were in their dens, possibly asleep. Not a threat. This was going to be so easy.

Staying in the safety of the darkness, she crept closer to the target. The scent of the hens and lambs was strong now. Her cubs would feed well tonight.

71

Chapter Six

Outfoxed

By the side of Peter's bed, Blue dozed, happily trapped in that magical moment between dream and awake. She yawned and stretched, lifting her back leg to gently scratch her ear. As she did so, she could have sworn she heard a low growling noise carried along by the breeze. She pricked her ears and sat bolt upright.

The outside winds were flowing into the room through the open window, bringing with them the secrets of the night.

Blue's nose tingled. She caught the faintest whiff of something strange. It was not a familiar scent … and it was definitely not a friendly one.

She ran to the window-sill, jumping up and resting her front paws on it. She leaned her head and nose out the window

and let out two muffled barks, just loud enough to wake her sleeping master.

'Blue,' groaned Peter, 'stop it, you'll wake everyone up.'

But Blue was not concerned about waking her humans. Her senses were telling her that something dangerous was out there, and she needed to get out – and get out fast.

The vixen studied the henhouse carefully. She pinned her nose to the ground and sniffed all along the base, looking for a way in. The walls were solid timber – no gaps to squeeze through like in other places. Feeling a little panicked, she paced back and forth. She would have to dig her way in.

Inside, Rodney felt her presence and began to fuss, puffing out his feathers and lifting his wings. The hens were in danger, and they were all trapped, with nowhere to run and no one to help them. Puffing out his chest for all he was worth, he did the one and only thing he could do ... Call for help.

COCKADOOODLE DOOOOOO000000oooooooo! he crowed with all his might.

COCKADOOODLE DOOOOOO000000oooooooo
COCKADOOODLE DOOOOOO000000oooooooo!

He caused great alarm in the henhouses, and the rest of the

hens began to cluck and squawk too.

Back in the house, Blue was also alarmed. On hearing Rodney's crows, she didn't need another warning. There was a trespasser – the animals were under threat. Yelping and barking, she scraped at the bedroom door. She had to get out, she had to help the animals.

Peter jumped up and threw on his clothes. He knew his dog sensed something, but he didn't want Blue to wake his parents up. They already didn't like her sleeping in his room, and if she woke them up, that would be it for sure.

He threw open his bedroom door and Blue dashed out, nearly flattening poor Kate, who was sleepily wandering back from the bathroom.

'Shhhhhh!' Peter whispered, before Kate could scream and cause even more commotion. 'Blue senses something outside, and I can hear noises coming from the Coopers' henhouse. I'm going to check it out.'

'Hettie,' mouthed Kate in alarm.

The little hen had not come when Kate called her earlier. Mam had told her not to worry, that hens enjoy being outdoors as the weather picks up. 'She'll find her own way home, you'll see,' Mam had said. 'We'll leave the shed door open so she can put herself to bed tonight.'

But Kate had a bad feeling, and now a deep dread and panic came over her.

'I'm coming too,' she whispered in a frantic tone. Running back to her room, she threw on some clothes and met her brother and Blue in the kitchen.

By now Blue was frantic. She was scratching at the back door, her nails leaving marks. She looked at her masters, begging them to let her out.

Grabbing a torch, Peter fumbled with the door key as Kate tried to keep Blue quiet.

CLICK!

The noise of the lock opening was almost deafening in the stillness of the house. The children looked at each other in panic – if their parents weren't awake by now, that would surely do it. They paused, but they couldn't hear any sounds from upstairs.

'Phew.' Peter let out a sigh of relief.

He opened the door. Blue burst out and ran towards the gap in the hedge that led to the Coopers' yard and the henhouse.

'Come on,' said Kate, her voice trembling. 'We'd better go too.'

Out they ran after Blue, into the dark night, slamming the door behind them.

* * *

Mam wasn't sure what had awoken her so abruptly. Had she heard a door slam and noises from the kitchen? She had a strange feeling that something was amiss.

'David,' she called, in a loud whisper. Her husband was gently snoring, enjoying a rare full night's sleep.

'David,' she called again, this time nudging him.

'Hmmmm. What is it?' he asked, a bit crossly.

'Did you hear that?'

'Hear what?'

'A door slam,' said Mam, throwing back the bed covers and heading for the hall.

Dad turned on the lamp and rubbed his eyes. 'It was probably a dream,' he said, hoping he could just lie back down and pick up his slumber from where he left off. 'We've been so busy with the lambing, we're all a bit on edge, I reckon.'

But Mam was not convinced. Opening the door, she stepped into the hallway, looking up and down and listening. It was very quiet. She headed for the children's bedrooms.

When her shrill screams rang out, Dad jumped out of bed.

'They're gone!' she shouted, running back to their room. 'The children are gone!'

The noise was deafening as the hens grew more and more distressed. The vixen was frantically digging, but she kept hitting solid stone. She couldn't get in, and by now that rooster had raised the alarm to mammoth levels.

She could hear a dog in the distance – this was too dangerous. It was time to move, time to get away.

* * *

The children followed Blue through the gap and straight to the henhouse. They heard the commotion inside. Peter shone his torch and could make out three little holes that were dug in the soft ground, wet from the night-time dew. There were paw prints all around them, paw prints that were too small to be Blue's. If anyone would know who or what made prints like these, it would be Kate.

'Kate!' he called. 'Look at these.'

Kate ran over and crouched low to the ground.

'I bet it's a fox,' she said, immediately alarmed, thinking about her beloved Hettie. She took Peter's torch and shone it along the timber walls. There were scratch marks too. 'It looks like it tried to scratch and dig its way in. I don't think it worked though.'

Kate shone the torch around some more.

Peter could read the worried look on his sister's face. 'Hettie is a clever hen,' he said gently. 'She can take care of herself.'

Suddenly, Blue's barks and whimpers startled them. They turned around to see her take off towards the meadow.

'Blue!' they called in unison, as she disappeared into the night.

Peter tried to whistle but it wasn't loud enough – he needed more practice.

'Where did she go?' cried Kate.

Her brother looked at her in fear. 'The lambs. Blue must be heading to the meadow.'

'Oh no!' wailed Kate, as they both sprinted away.

Over at Cooper's Cottage, the racket from the henhouse had also woken Maggie and Eamon.

'What is making all that noise?' Maggie exclaimed, going to the bedroom window and pulling back the curtains.

Eamon was already throwing on his work clothes over his checked pyjamas. He dashed for the hallway with Maggie following close behind him. He went to the special safe that was hidden inside the hallway cupboard, unlocked it, and grabbed his shotgun.

'You stay here,' he said to Maggie.

Maggie nodded and put her hand to her mouth. She was worried, and if the truth be known, quite frightened. 'Be careful, my love,' she called out after her husband.

Eamon hurried out of the house and towards the henhouse. His years of experience with animals told him that something big must be happening to cause such a raucous.

All kinds of thoughts were running through his mind. *Could it be a fox or a mink after the hens? Or was it an ...* Suddenly, in the distance, he saw something moving towards him, a torch light bouncing up and down.

... an intruder.

'Who's there?' Eamon shouted, raising the shotgun as he did so.

'It's only me, Eamon!' Dad called out. 'The children have gone missing. Have you seen them? Blue's gone too.'

Eamon's eyes grew wide in shock. It was far too late and far too dark for the children to be out alone.

'Don't worry, David,' he said, trying to keep his voice calm. 'We'll find them. They can't be gone far, and if Blue's with them, they'll be ok. Something has been disturbing the hens. Maybe it's the children.'

The two men ran towards the henhouse. By now the hens were starting to settle down, but there was no sign of the children or Blue anywhere.

'They're not here,' said Dad. Now feeling really panicked, he reached for his phone. 'I'll have to call Marian. We need the police.'

But Eamon had spotted something. 'Hold on. They're not here now, but they were ... Look!'

He shone his torch along the ground as Dad crouched down. In the mud, they could make out footprints with a large star shape in the middle.

'I'd recognise the sole of Kate's welly boots anywhere!' said Dad.

Along the ground, they also picked up Peter's boot prints and Blue's paw prints.

And that wasn't all.

Dad's torch lit up three freshly dug holes at the side of the henhouse and more animal prints dotted around. He moved in for a closer look. 'These are too small to be Blue's. Could there be a cat?'

But Eamon knew it was no cat. 'A fox,' he snarled. 'It's no wonder Rodney has been so fussy lately. I'd say my hens have been under watch for some time.'

They checked the area for more clues. There were scratches along the walls, as if the fox had tried to claw its way inside.

'It doesn't look like it got in,' said Dad. 'It must have been very angry to leave scratches like these.'

'This henhouse has concrete foundations,' said Eamon with pride. 'A fox could have the strength to dig all the way to China, and they still wouldn't get in.'

But Dad wasn't listening. *Where could the children be?* He shone his torch across the fence and towards his own house and fields. 'Peter, Kate!' he called out. 'Peter, Kate, where are you?'

He reached for his phone again and called home, telling a frantic Mam that they may need to call the police.

As he spoke, Eamon's ears picked up the sound of muffled barks in the distance. He twirled around to Dad. 'Shhhhh!' He put his fingers to his lips. 'Do you hear that?'

Dad took the phone away from his ear. Mam's sobs could be heard on the other end.

The two men listened, hardly daring to breathe. It was Blue, they were sure of it. She was barking, letting them know her location … All of a sudden, it hit them. *The sheep!*

'Don't worry, Marian,' Dad assured Mam. 'I think we know where they are.' He hung up the phone and took off in the direction of the sheep meadow.

Despite his older years and holding a heavy gun, Eamon managed to keep up. They followed the sound of Blue's barking, hoping that wherever she was, the children were there too.

Chapter Seven

Strong Stock

The vixen was annoyed that there would be no chickens for her cubs. That dog had ruined her plans, and what were those two small humans doing? At least there were plenty of lambs here – if she acted fast, she could easily bring back two. She was always one step ahead, always cleverer. In the distance, she could hear barking. The dog was getting closer, so there was no time to hesitate, no time to waste.

Creeping under the fence, she used her senses to track her prey. Her eyes, fully adjusted to the darkness, could make out the clusters of sheep dotted around the meadow. Her nose filled with their scent, and her stomach rumbled in anticipation. If she was going to get away with this, she would need to grab and dash, choosing only those sheep close to the fence.

Suddenly she spotted her prey: a ewe with two lambs. Surely the sheep wouldn't miss one? And there was another ewe sleeping, her two lambs snuggled up next to her. This was really too easy.

With a low growl, the vixen made a dash straight for the unsuspecting sheep.

BUMPF!!

Out of nowhere, she was thrown to the ground, as if she had been hit by a tornado. She staggered up, dazed. She turned to see the dog standing between her and her prey. The dog was snarling, its head low and eyes steadily fixed on her. It arched its back, ready to attack again.

With gunshots and humans behind her and a dog in front of her, the vixen was cornered. Left with no other option, she had to fight back.

She charged straight at the dog, throwing her full weight against Blue's side and knocking her to the ground, stunned. Seeing her chance, the vixen bit down hard, shaking her head, tearing the skin and flesh.

Blue yelped in pain. She managed to turn sharply, throwing the vixen down again before collapsing to the ground.

Back on the path, the children heard Blue's yelp. It ripped through the night and rang in their ears. Kate screamed.

'Blue!' Peter shouted, his heart pounding as his legs tried to get him to the meadow as quickly as possible. Finally, he and Kate reached the gate.

'You stay here,' Peter shouted to his sister as he climbed over and jumped down on the other side.

Further away, Dad and Eamon heard Blue's yelp too.

'Did you hear that?' Dad shouted. 'And I heard Kate screaming.'

'They must be in trouble,' said Eamon. He raised his gun, letting off a shot into the sky.

The vixen flinched at the sound of gunshot, her instincts telling her she was beaten. With the dog lying on the ground, it was her chance to get away. She swung around sharply, away from those that threatened her, and dived back under the fence. She crossed the field and ran for the safety of her den. Earlier, she had picked up the scent of a rabbit – that will have to do for dinner.

Dad and Eamon arrived at the meadow gate just as the vixen disappeared over the hill.

Kate was already there, her face in her hands, her shoulders hunched and shaking as she wept.

'Kate.' Dad grabbed her in his arms. 'Are you ok?'

'Oh Dad,' she sobbed, her face covered in tears. 'It's awful. Blue's hurt, and I can't see Peter.'

Leaving his gun with Dad, Eamon climbed over the gate and ran into the meadow, calling for Peter. He shone his torch to the far end of the field. The sheep were huddled together, frightened. He brought the light forward to where Blue was lying. She wasn't moving. Peter was next to her, his head low and his tears flowing fast.

'Oh no,' Eamon said under his breath. 'Oh please, no.'

He placed his hand on Peter's shoulder. Peter didn't even notice. He was too focused on Blue, who was lying so still and so quiet.

'It's ok, girl,' Peter whispered. He looked up at Eamon. 'She will be ok, won't she?'

Eamon placed his hand along Blue's neck, feeling something wet and warm. 'Peter, she's bleeding,' he said, trying not to sound as panicked as he felt. He then ran his hand along her back and over her heart. 'A heartbeat. Thank goodness, I can feel her heartbeat.'

Eamon took off his coat, paying no attention to the night's cool air. He wrapped it around the injured dog, picked her up gently and turned for home.

Peter jumped up, running his sleeved hand under his nose. 'You did so well, Blue,' he whispered in her ear. 'So brave.'

Eamon felt a lump rise in his throat. He had been so hard on this dog, so quick to judge her, and now look what had happened. She had put her life on the line to protect the flock.

'You hang in there, girl,' Eamon whispered. 'Your mum would be so proud of what you did tonight.'

Eamon cradled the injured dog as they reached the fence, where Dad and Kate were waiting. Mam was there too, unable to stay home one more minute. Kate was clinging to her parents.

Peter ran to his mother. 'Please, Mam,' he wailed, 'you have

to save her. You have to save Blue.'

Mam stepped towards Eamon, who opened his coat to show her Blue's wound. It was deep, and Blue was losing a lot of blood.

'I need her in my surgery,' Mam said to Eamon, trying to keep her voice steady so as not to frighten the children. In a more hushed tone to Eamon, she mouthed, 'We need her there *now*.'

As the others went back to the house with Blue, Dad, still holding Eamon's gun, checked on the flock. Thankfully no sheep were stuck in the ditches or lying on their backs unable to get up. Some were starting to graze again, and the lambs were taking milk. Blue had saved them. She had saved them all. But could they save Blue?

He shot into the night sky once more. Hopefully the gunshot and their lingering scents would be enough to deter the fox from returning tonight.

Eamon placed Blue gently on the steel surgery table, leaving his coat underneath her to keep her warm. Blue's eyes had opened a few minutes ago, but she was very weak. She panted softly, allowing her eyelids to droop every now and again.

In the brightly lit surgery, Mam was able to examine the

89

wound properly. As she feared, it was deep, causing Blue to bleed heavily. Blue's flesh had been badly torn, which would make it difficult to clean and stitch. There might also be damage to the muscle – they wouldn't know for sure until Blue started to move, but for now every movement was a huge effort for her and a risk of further injury.

Mam was also worried about infection. There was a chance that this fox might carry a disease, and what had Blue been lying on in the meadow? Diseases, parasites and other infections were common on a farm and a risk to even healthy animals. If Blue had been exposed, she may be in even more trouble.

As Eamon moved his hand away, fresh blood oozed and ran onto the table. He glanced up at Mam, who took a handful of gauze and pressed it hard against Blue's neck to stop the flow. Eamon took over, allowing Mam to fill a small needle. It was medicine to help Blue relax and sleep. Mam injected Blue and waited for her eyes to close and her panting to slow.

'Time for Blue to rest,' she said to Peter, who stood at the door of the surgery, his wide eyes filled with tears and utter confusion.

* * *

In the kitchen, Maggie had arrived armed with scones and strawberry jam. 'You must all be so hungry,' she said, reaching for the kettle.

Mam, Eamon and Peter were still in the surgery with Blue, and Dad was at the meadow. Poor Kate sat alone, curled up in an armchair. She was normally so strong and confident – seemingly older than her eight years – but now she looked lost and frightened. Her little face was pale, her eyes sunken and red from the tears that wouldn't stop flowing.

'Oh, Maggie,' she whimpered, 'it was awful. I've never heard Blue cry like that, and I don't know where Hettie is. I looked everywhere, but …' Unable to finish before the tears started again, Kate dropped her face into her hands.

Maggie rushed over and took the little girl in a warm embrace. 'There, there, my little Kate,' she whispered. 'Blue is in the best possible hands, and as for Miss Hettie, she'll be back, you just wait and see.'

Larry, who was lying in his basket and wondering why he wasn't getting any attention, looked over at Maggie and Kate and let out a plaintive *baaaaa baaaa*.

'Don't you start,' scolded Maggie. 'All my hugs are for this little one.'

* * *

Peter went over to Blue after Mam had given her the injection. 'Have a nice sleep, Blue,' he whispered in her ear. 'You'll be feeling better in no time.'

His voice choked, and two tear puddles landed on the table.

'It's ok, pet,' said Mam, who was pressing Blue's wound with fresh gauze. 'Go on into the kitchen. By the sounds of it, Maggie has arrived and no doubt there will be some treats.'

'Aye lad,' said Eamon. 'Let's leave your Mam to work her magic.'

Peter looked desperately at his mother. 'Please Mam,' he sniffed, 'I ... I ... I can't leave her.'

Mam and Eamon exchanged a glance. 'He can stay here,' she said to Eamon. And then to Peter, 'You can stay, but you must stand back, ok?'

Eamon smiled. *That boy really loves that dog*, he thought to himself. *What a special bond they have. The kind that happens once in a lifetime.*

Suddenly, Eamon understood why Blue hadn't performed her best at the test trial that morning. She needed to hear the commands from her true master, Peter, not him. Blue's instincts tonight to protect the herd were the signs of a top-class working dog. He could see that now. Eamon had had his glory days with Peg, and now it was time for the next generation to take over.

'We will get you right as rain, Blue,' he said quietly, 'and then we'll make you the champion you proved yourself to be tonight.'

With Eamon gone and Peter sitting quietly against the wall, Mam got to work. She clipped the hair on Blue's neck, trying to clear as much of the area as she could without causing more damage.

'She's going to need stitches, a lot of stitches,' Mam muttered to herself.

She washed out the wound and quickly started stitching, already thinking about the antibiotics Blue would need and what to do if there was muscle or tendon damage.

With tears in his eyes, Peter watched his mother at work.

* * *

Meanwhile, back in the kitchen, Maggie had made a fresh pot of tea for the grownups, warm cocoa for Kate, and a bottle of milk for the cheeky little lamb. Larry's suckling noises lightened the mood and brought a smile back to Kate's tear-stained face.

Dad arrived home from the fields and looked straight at Eamon. 'Well?' he asked.

'Your Marian's working on Blue,' Eamon said, shaking his head. 'She's in a bad way, David.'

Maggie touched Eamon's arm. 'She's from strong stock, that Blue,' she whispered to him. 'She'll fight this.'

Eamon nodded, saying a little prayer under his breath.

* * *

When she was finished stitching and cleaning the wound, Mam moved Blue to a small area covered with shredded newspapers. Blue was still out cold, and even though Mam had given her painkillers, she would be uncomfortable and sore when she awoke.

'Blue will be staying here tonight,' Mam said to Peter, who still hadn't moved. 'We'll know more in the morning.'

'Can I sleep here?' Peter asked, already knowing the answer.

'No,' said Mam, pointing to the door. 'You need your sleep too, young man.'

Peter knew not to argue, and he headed towards the door, leaving his mother behind to clean up.

It was now late, well past midnight. At least it was Sunday, and he didn't have to think about school.

Upstairs, Dad was tucking Kate into bed. Maggie's cocoa and scones had worked their magic, and she could hardly keep her eyes open any longer.

'Dad,' she said sleepily, 'I couldn't find Hettie. Do you think the fox got her?'

Her father tried his best to smile reassuringly. He stroked her hair as he searched for the right words.

'Now is not the time to worry about Hettie,' he whispered. 'She has her ways and is a very clever hen. I am sure she is fine.'

94

He leaned in and kissed Kate gently on the cheek. She smiled and turned over, finally ready to give in to slumber.

Dad sat on the bed for a while until he was sure Kate was settled. As he left, he turned back to look upon the sleeping child before switching out the light and closing the door. He went downstairs to the kitchen, hoping that Maggie had another pot of tea on the go. Despite his brave words, he couldn't help but worry a little about Hettie.

Wherever you are, little hen, he thought, *get yourself home safe.*

The grandfather clock in the hallway chimed 2am. The adults were still sitting in the kitchen together, drinking endless pots of tea and talking about the night's events. They knew only too well how awful things could have been had it not been for the bravery of the children and Blue.

Peter slept in an armchair in the corner, and Larry dozed in his basket by the stove.

Eamon nodded over to the little lamb. 'He's doing well,' he said to Dad. 'By the looks of it, he's ready to go back.'

'As long as we haven't left it too long,' Dad replied. 'I had hoped that ewe would've lambed by now, but she's not ready to go yet.'

'Don't worry, David,' Eamon said, with a smile. 'Mother nature has her ways. It will happen, and when it does, I must show you the trick my dad taught me when it came to fostering lambs. It never failed him, and it won't fail this little one either.'

Dad wasn't sure, but he appreciated Eamon's confidence. 'Maybe you'll come by tomorrow, then. Check her over and tell me more about this trick of your dad's.'

Eamon nodded, happy to help.

'David,' said Maggie, 'I don't suppose you saw any sign of Hettie while checking the flock?'

'No,' said Dad, 'and Kate was asking me if I thought the fox had got her.'

'She is so sensitive about the animals,' said Mam, with a worried frown. 'I've been trying to tell her that Hettie will find her way back, but to be honest, it does seem strange that she's missing for so long.'

The adults went silent for a moment, the ticking of the grandfather clock suddenly reminding them of the late hour.

'Ok, it's time we headed for home,' said Maggie, bringing the plates and cups to the sink. 'Tomorrow is another day. My father always said a sunrise is a blank page to write a new adventure.'

The clinking of the dishes woke Peter. 'Blue,' he muttered sleepily.

'She's doing fine,' said Mam. 'She's still sleeping off the anaesthesia. As for you, you should be sleeping too, and not just in a chair. Come on, I'll tuck you in.'

'Goodnight, Peter,' said Eamon, draining the end of his tea. 'Sleep tight. Your Blue will need you to be at your best tomorrow.'

Maggie caught Peter in one of her ginormous hugs. 'You three were quite the team tonight,' she said. 'I'll have to make something extra special for the treat tin.'

Even though he thought he would be flattened by the strength of her embrace, Peter felt better, and for the briefest of moments, he forgot about his worry for Blue.

Chapter Eight

All Sheeps and Sizes

The next morning dawned bright and sunny. For many people, Sundays are a day of rest – but not for farmers. Dad was up before first light, checking the sheep in the meadow again. He had hardly slept a wink thinking about what might have happened to his flock if it wasn't for Blue and the children. He would spend the day putting in extra protection, but right now, there was another important job to take care of.

In the shed, he saw that, finally, the ewe he hoped would adopt Larry was showing signs she was ready to

lamb. She was pawing at the ground and making circles in the straw. She had made herself a small nest, and after getting up and down numerous times, she was finally staying down.

Not only was this ewe an experienced and gentle mother, but a vet's scan early on in her pregnancy showed she was carrying just one lamb. She could handle a second one no problem, so there was a greater chance for a little orphan to be adopted. On paper, she was perfect – but Dad knew that with nature, nothing was ever certain.

He had already placed Larry in a small pen close to the door of the shed. He wanted him to be free from the scent of humans, which might be off-putting for the ewe. As if he knew, the little lamb started jumping and hopping and rolling in the fresh straw straight away. Larry had thrived under Mam's expert care, but now, hopefully, he was ready to join a family of his own.

'Are you there, David?'

Eamon's arrival couldn't have been better timed, and Dad was happy to see him. He respected Eamon's opinions and trusted his instincts. Dad had spent his whole life on a farm, but there was always more to learn.

Eamon was carrying a kettle of water, a sponge, a carton of salt, and a large bucket. The steam from the kettle puffed with each step he took. He walked to the pen and stood beside Dad. The ewe was now panting heavily, her labour well under way. Her own little lamb would soon be here.

'You stay with the little ram,' Eamon said, nodding over to Larry. 'I'll stay here and help our latest mum to be.'

Eamon walked slowly to the back of the ewe. It was important not to go too fast and startle or stress the sheep, but this was like second nature to Eamon, and in no time, he was in position and ready to help should it be needed.

From the rear of the ewe suddenly appeared what looked like a bubble of water. As it emerged, it grew larger and then suddenly burst and spilt its watery contents over the straw bed. This bag of fluid was the first sign that the new lamb was on its way, and it was a vital ingredient for Eamon's plan.

'We will be needing some of that for Larry's adoption,' he said with a knowing smile, as he used the sponge to gather as much of the fluid as he could into the bucket. His own father was an experienced sheep farmer; being able to carry on his farming methods made Eamon feel close to him, like he was still there beside him.

Suddenly Dad understood what Eamon was doing. By covering Larry with the ewe's birthing fluids, she might think she had just given birth to him. Eamon would also cover him with warm, salty water – this would ensure that Larry's body temperature was the same as if he had just been born, and the salt would encourage the ewe to lick him and bond with him.

All of these tricks would help, but the final part of the process could not be influenced by Dad or Eamon. If the ewe's own mothering instincts weren't triggered, there was nothing they or anyone else could do about it.

Careful not to disturb her, Eamon placed his items near the ewe, who was now standing. The bucket containing its magical contents had to be close at hand and used quickly if this was to have any chance at all.

By now, two small legs had appeared from the rear of the ewe. Eamon took hold of them and gently pulled towards him. The legs were soon followed by a nose, a head – and with one final push, the new lamb slipped free from its mother. As it lay strewn across the straw, Eamon picked it up by its back legs and lay it close to its mother, whose instincts were already at work. She began licking it frantically, removing the mucus and fluid from its nose and mouth, bringing it fully to life and ready to take its first steps.

As she continued to lick and nibble at her newly born lamb, Eamon put his plan into action. He scooped up the straw that the lamb had been lying on – it was vital to get as much of its scent as possible. He poured some salt and some warm water from the kettle into the bucket.

'I promise you, lad,' Eamon said to Dad, 'this will work.'

Dad took Larry in his arms and placed him straight into the bucket, drenching him in all the fluids. He and Eamon rubbed the straw all over his little body, then placed the now sodden Larry near the ewe.

The two men stepped away and held their breaths.

With the mucus now fully cleaned from its nose and mouth, the newborn lamb shook its head, scattering droplets as it did so. It was not long before it attempted to move towards its mother, hungry and driven by the need to feed. It staggered with its early steps and reached up to take its first drink and fill its tiny body with nutritious colostrum.

With her own lamb clean and fed, the ewe looked behind her to see yet another warm, wet little creature lying on the straw. She gingerly sniffed and nudged Larry before instinctively reaching down and licking him, just as she had her other lamb.

Baaaa! Larry shook his wet body and, picking up the scent of milk, he copied the other lamb by heading to the ewe's udder for a drink of his own.

Dad bit his lip. This was the moment. There was every chance the ewe would reject the little lamb. But no, she simply turned her head and stood still, allowing this second lamb to drink his fill.

As Larry finished, she turned and rubbed him with her nose, showing that she had accepted him as her own. Even though he was nearly two days older than the other lamb, Larry was still quite small, and when viewed side by side, the two lambs could easily have been mistaken for twins.

A large grin spread across Eamon's face. He patted Dad on the shoulder.

'Now all is as it should be,' said Dad, relieved.

Larry took another drink and then lay down next to his new mother and sister. The ewe turned her head and nuzzled the little lambs, one after the other.

Dad's own belly began to rumble. 'Right, time for my breakfast too!'

Eamon waved him on, more than happy to clean up and take over.

On the walk home, Dad realised how exhausted he was. He was grateful for the chance to switch off, even if it was only for a short while. They were only halfway through what had already been a very eventful lambing season. It would be another few weeks before they were done, and Dad was looking forward to the start of summer when the ewes and their youngsters could relax and graze on the sweet May grass.

Back at the kitchen table, the children were all a-chatter about the previous night's drama. When Dad arrived, they momentarily stopped and looked up, eager to hear about Larry. When they didn't see him in their father's arms, smiles ran across their faces.

'It worked, didn't it?' beamed Kate, punching the air. She

was sad at the thought of Larry going away to join a flock, but she understood that it was the best thing for him.

'Shhhhh!' Peter put his finger to his lips. 'Blue,' he mouthed, pointing in the direction of Mam's surgery at the back of the house.

Kate rolled her eyes. 'She'll never hear us from all the way back there, Peter.'

Dad smiled, nodded his head and gave a thumbs up. 'Larry and his new sister are getting to know each other, and so far, all is working out just fine.'

The children were glad to hear about Larry's new family, although the kitchen seemed so much quieter without him.

'Can we go see them?' Peter pleaded.

'After breakfast,' said Mam, walking into the kitchen. She had been checking on Blue. 'I'm sure they will be happy to have visitors then. And anyway, there's someone closer to home who might enjoy some visitors right now.'

'Blue!' Peter exclaimed, forgetting about his whisper rule. The children jumped up from their chairs.

Mam raised her hands to slow them down. 'But not for too long! She's awake and her eyes are bright, but she has a long way to go yet.'

Peter dashed out of the room, but Kate paused, looking at the back door. 'Hettie should be here by now,' she said to no one in particular. She turned to Dad. 'Did you see her?'

Dad shook his head. 'No, pet. But that doesn't mean something bad has happened.'

'Exactly,' said Mam, trying to smile. 'After you spend some time with Blue, we'll go on a little search party for Hettie. No doubt she is up to some kind of mischief, completely unaware of how worried we all are.'

Feeling better, Kate spun on her heels and followed her brother in to see Blue.

'It will break her heart if something has happened to that hen,' whispered Dad.

'We'll just have to distract her,' said Mam. 'I'll make sure she is there to help me with Blue's recovery.'

'How long will that take?' asked Dad.

'Hard to say,' answered Mam. 'If the medication does what it is supposed to do, it could be three to four weeks. But … well, she's not out of the woods yet.'

Blue lifted her head when she saw the children. As they knelt down beside her, she lay her head on Peter's lap, exhausted by even that small movement.

'You'll be ok, Blue,' Peter said, stroking her ears. He was careful not to touch the bandaged area on her neck. Blue closed her eyes again, happy to have the children close by.

'You are the bravest, bestest dog ever,' Kate whispered, and gave her a gentle kiss.

Blue's tail made a small movement, enough to show the children that she was happy and not in too much pain. Her breathing was still quite laboured, though, and occasionally she made a little grunting noise.

The trio remained like this for a short while, Blue lost somewhere between awake and asleep, and the children careful not to upset or harm her in any way. Their strokes were slow and careful, and their words quiet and loving.

'Ok, you two, that's enough for now,' Mam said, standing in the doorway. 'Blue needs a lot of rest. Why don't we leave her alone and take a walk outside?'

The children reluctantly followed their mother's instructions.

'She's looking much better,' said Peter, giving Mam a big hug. 'Thank you, thank you so much.'

Not wanting to be left out, Kate joined in the group hug. She buried her face into her mother's side. 'You saved her, Mam. You saved Blue.'

The children didn't see a small tear roll down their mother's face. 'You're so very welcome' was all she could say, overcome with emotion.

Even though the sun was shining on this March morning, there was a cold breeze that held a reminder of winter in its chill. Wrapping up, Peter, Kate and their parents went outside and walked towards Cooper's Farm. On the way, they stopped in to see Larry and meet his new family.

Baaaaaaaaaa! The little lamb called out when he saw them.

'He still remembers us!' said Peter.

'Of course he does,' said Kate. 'It's only been a day, you know.'

'Keep back, Peter,' said Dad. 'They are still bonding, and I don't want any mixed signals to get in the way.'

Peter nodded and stood next to his dad, who explained how he and Eamon had helped Larry meet his new family. Kate listened too, but she kept looking towards the door, trying to catch a glimpse of Hettie or hear her familiar clucking. She hadn't returned home, and even though Kate's parents kept saying everything was ok, she was not feeling so sure.

After visiting Larry, they made their way towards Cooper's Cottage, where they saw a car parked at the entrance gate. A figure in a large hat, long coat and sunglasses was scurrying around to the driver's side, arms laden with egg boxes.

'What's going on there?' asked Dad. 'That person is behaving rather oddly.'

Kate looked in the back window and recognised a girl from her class. 'It's Karen Reilly,' she said, waving in.

Karen glanced over at Kate, then snapped her head back around, completely ignoring her.

'Oh, she's so snooty!' Kate snarled.

The figure with the eggs looked around. It was Karen's mother, Monica Reilly. She was buying eggs from Maggie's honesty box!

'Why is Mrs Reilly getting some of Maggie's eggs?' asked Peter. 'Don't they have their own?'

'I thought their eggs were the *best ones around*!' Kate said, mimicking Karen Reilly's voice.

'I think we've just caught out the Reillys!' laughed Dad.

'Morning, Karen!' Kate called out.

'Morning, Monica!' said Mam, throwing her a big smile and waving.

'Eh, morning,' Mrs Reilly answered, blushing as she did. 'Morning, Marian. Lovely day, isn't it?'

'Glorious,' Mam answered. 'Buying eggs for some home baking?'

'Cooper's Farm Eggs make the spongiest sponge around,' added Kate.

'Don't be so cheeky, Kate,' whispered Mam, trying not to laugh.

Monica Reilly didn't answer. She clambered back into her car and pulled away (at some speed, it must be said), with both occupants staring straight ahead.

'You two are as bad as Maggie,' Dad said, giving Mam a gentle nudge.

'I couldn't resist,' giggled Mam.

Just then, Eamon came out of the house. 'I thought I heard voices,' he said as he strolled towards them.

The children wasted no time in telling him about Blue and how she was doing a little better, and about Larry, who was still delighted with his new family.

'But we can't find Hettie,' added Kate. 'Have you or Maggie seen her?'

'Well, no, not today,' said Eamon. 'Why don't we head over to the henhouse? I'll be letting the girls out to stretch their legs and get some exercise. It'll do them the world of good after the nasty business of last night. Maybe all their clucking will bring Hettie back.'

On their way to the henhouse, they looked for clues that could help with finding Hettie – or could show if the fox had made a return.

'Here's a fox print!' shouted Peter excitedly, taking a magnifying glass out of his pocket.

'That's it, Sherlock Holmes,' laughed Eamon. 'Follow the clues.'

'There's another,' cried Kate.

Peter ran to where his sister was, then followed the tracks to the back of the henhouse and towards the fence. Stooping down, he noticed a clump of feathers. They were cream with brown speckles. There was only one cream and brown speckled hen Peter knew of.

Oh no, he thought.

'HETTIE!' Kate screamed.

Mam and Dad ran to her side, and Eamon followed. Through her sobs, Kate pointed to the small pile of feathers.

'I don't remember seeing these last night,' said Eamon, scratching his head.

They searched high and low, but Hettie was nowhere to be found. No traces at all except for the scattering of feathers beside the fence. Maybe the vixen had a victory after all and brought a hen home for dinner.

Over in the Coopers' kitchen, Maggie was hugging Kate, who hadn't stopped crying. She was still clutching Hettie's feathers, all she had left to remind her of her little friend. Not even Maggie's treat tin could help.

'Now, now,' said Maggie, trying to console her. 'You have all your lambs, and in a few days, we will have more little chicks. Our lives will be full of new life.'

'Won't that be something to look forward to?' asked Mam hopefully. 'You can also help me get Blue back to her full, happy and healthy self.'

But no matter how hard they tried to make Kate feel better, her heart was broken. There was no other hen – or animal, for that matter – that would ever take Hettie's place. She was so special. Hettie had been Kate's very first pet, and from the moment that little fluffball hopped into her outstretched hand, Kate's heart had swelled. Nothing could, nor ever would, replace her. *Nothing.*

Chapter Nine

Fluffballs

As the weeks went by, new life was everywhere. Early April showers gave way to milder, drier days, which were welcomed by the growing animal population of Hazel Tree. Lambing season would soon be over, and summer would finally begin. The young lambs were taking full advantage of the warmer days, playing together happily in the meadow. The happiest of all was Larry, whose new mother protected and loved him like her own.

In the days after the vixen attack, Dad and Eamon had been busy coming up with new ways to safeguard the livestock. The henhouse had successfully protected the hens indoors, so they put up electrified mesh fencing for when all the animals were outside. Fox-repellent oils were put on all the new lambs, and Dad installed a lighting system that gave the impression of torch light at night-time. No fox would enter a field if they thought a farmer was roaming amongst the flock.

The local farmers in Ballynoe had been kind, sharing their own sheepdogs, giving lots of good advice, and helping Dad to put the new security in place.

One thing was for sure: Blue was hailed as a hero and a dog of great instincts. Since that fateful night, there had been no other major emergencies or dramas. They had won, and the vixen had lost.

By now the chicks had also arrived at Cooper's Farm. Even though they were only a couple of weeks old, they were already out and about, scratching and pecking – but never straying too far from the ever-watchful eyes of the mother hens.

Maggie took care to involve Kate as much as possible with the new chicks. Kate had smiled when she heard the little beaks tapping away on the inside of the eggs and smiled a little more as they cracked and burst through the shells. Newly hatched, the chicks were wet and slimy, but within a short period of time their feathers dried, transforming them into little yellow and brown fluffballs. Their chirping was like a chorus, and they were the cutest things ever. But although Maggie meant well, it made Kate sad when she was given a chick to hold. It reminded her too much of Hettie.

As Kate continued to mourn her little hen, back at the house, Blue's recovery had been slow but steady. Overall, she was doing well, but a small infection a week in had set her back and caused Peter some worry.

'It'll be ok, Peter,' Mam had reassured him. 'Another course of antibiotics will have her recovery back on track.'

Mam was expecting some complications along the way. Blue's injuries were serious, but her youth as well as the love and care of those around her had all done so much to bring this girl back to herself.

Peter visited Blue every day, filling her in on all the latest news from the farm. He told her how well Larry and the other lambs were doing and let her know if any chicks had hatched that day. She whined a little whenever he mentioned Hettie, as if to tell Peter she was sad her little friend was no longer there.

When the time came to remove Blue's stitches, Peter and Kate patted and soothed her while their mother snipped the threads. With great care, Mam gently tugged until each loop was gone. Blue's fur had been clipped for hygiene, so once the stitches were out, it was easy to see how well they had helped the skin knit back together and close over the open wound. Blue still had a long red gash, which looked painful. Peter winced when he saw it and was glad when Mam cleaned the area again and put a fresh bandage back on.

'We'll need to change that every day for the next week,' Mam said.

'I can do it,' said Kate.

'No, I'd like to do it,' said Peter.

Something told Kate not to argue with her brother on this one.

Under his mother's guidance, and true to his word, Peter

changed and cleaned Blue's wound daily. When it began to scab over and heal further, Peter was delighted.

Now, nearly five weeks since that awful night, all that remained were the memories and a long pink scar that would soon be completely hidden under Blue's freshly grown fur.

In the early days of her recovery, Blue had been happy to stay in the house and not stray too far, but as she started to feel better, she grew restless and a little bit boisterous, stealing socks from the laundry and gnawing on chair legs. Every now and again, she would bark and whimper and scratch at the door.

'I've just brought you out for a wee!' Peter would say, a bit annoyed.

But Mam knew what those signs meant, and she was delighted to see them. What Blue needed now was to be back outside – fresh air, sunshine and exercise would complete the recovery process. But the timing would have to be just right.

One morning in mid-April, Mam looked out the window and knew that today was the day. It was warm, with the promise of May in the air. 'I think you can take Blue out for a proper walk,' she said to the children as they munched their breakfast.

'Do you think she's ready to start training again?' asked Peter excitedly. It was four months until Ballynoe Fair, and he hoped there was still enough time to get Blue ready to compete in the sheepdog trials.

'Take her slowly, Peter,' warned Mam. 'Bring her back gently, and don't expect too much too soon. Eamon will guide you.'

* * *

On the farm, Dad was as busy as always. Even though lambing season was over, there were plenty of jobs that needed doing: animals to be fed, sheds to be cleaned out, and machinery to be checked and serviced.

As he crossed the yard with a bucket in each hand, he suddenly stopped in his tracks. His jaw dropped.

'What on earth …' he cried out in disbelief.

An unbelievable sight was making its way to the back door of their farmhouse.

PECK PECK PECK

Having her breakfast, Kate thought she was hearing things. She looked over at Mam, who was staring back at her, her eyes wide with amazement. Blue's ears pricked up, and Peter paused mid chew on his jam and toast.

Surely they all weren't hearing things!

Kate rose from her chair and went to the back door. Slowly she opened it, looked out and looked down. She couldn't believe her eyes. Standing there was none other than Hettie the hen.

And she was not alone …

One, two, three, four, five, SIX little chicks in tow.

The children gasped as Hettie paused for a moment before stepping into the kitchen. By the way she was acting, you would not think she had been missing for over a month! Showing off her new babies, Hettie strolled proudly past an astonished Kate, her little chicks close behind.

'Oh Hettie!' cried Kate. 'Mam, look, it's Hettie! Can you believe it? She's here, and she's a mum!'

'Well, I never.' Mam was amazed. 'She must have sensed there was danger on the farm and chose to hatch her chicks somewhere safer. By the looks of them, they're at least a week old.'

'Beautiful, clever Hettie,' Kate said, reaching down to snuggle her little pal.

Chirp, chirp, chirp came the chorus of chicks, who ran over to investigate.

'You're going to have to put more bedding in that shed,' said Dad, who was standing at the door, the two buckets still in his hands.

'And I don't think crumbs and crusts from the table will be enough for this lot!' added a delighted Mam.

Kate beamed. 'No problem! I can get more straw from the sheep shed, and do you think Maggie and Eamon will give me some extra chicken feed?'

'Oh, I think that could be arranged,' said Mam, delighted to see her little girl smiling again. She reached into the cupboard

and took out a box of porridge oatlets. 'Here, this will keep them going until we get some chick crumb from Maggie.'

A beaming Kate took the box.

They'll need something for their water too, Mam thought to herself.

She went back to the presses and pulled out two plastic plates the children had used when they were little. They had curved sides that were high enough to hold water but low enough for the chicks to reach it without falling in.

Perfect, she thought and handed them to Kate.

'These are perfect for holding water,' Kate said, reading her mother's mind.

Mam laughed. Her daughter had natural instincts for animal care. She would make a great vet one day.

With everything they needed, Blue and Peter, Kate, Hettie and the chicks all headed outside. Blue wagged her tail, happy to be back in the middle of the action. Hettie, the protective mama hen, fussed over her babies and fluttered up her wings if she felt anyone was getting too close to them.

Peter and Kate got more straw to bed down Hettie's shed, creating a cosy little nest for the adorable brood. They poured some of the porridge oatlets on the ground, which were pecked up with great enthusiasm. Kate gently put down the plates of water, doing her best not to spill any, just as Maggie arrived with some chick crumb. Mam had called her with the news, and it was obvious she had rushed over – her face was flushed but her eyes were sparkling.

'Perfect, just perfect!' Maggie exclaimed as she took in the wonderful sight before her. 'What a clever girl you are, Miss Hettie.'

Summer finally arrived and brought with it long, warm days for the humans and animals at Hazel Tree. The children spent as much time as possible outdoors, helping Blue get stronger and keeping an eye out for any more vixens that might come calling. Dad and Eamon had worked hard improving security, but the children knew how clever a fox could be, especially a fox on the hunt.

Hettie was a dedicated mother. She fussed over her chicks, making sure none of them wandered off alone or near the other hens.

Maggie had given Kate proper drinkers and enough feed to keep the brood going for months. She explained to Kate how to mind the little ones and how she should only let them out for a short while each day, until they were bigger and stronger.

'Hettie already trusts you,' Maggie told her, with a tone of caution, 'but she will be protective, so approach carefully and watch out if you see her puffing her feathers and flapping her wings. That's her instinct, and it shows what a good mum she is.'

As the chicks got older, they were happy running around the backyard, throwing up dust on their adult feathers in the summer sun. By the start of June, they were already eight weeks old and showing signs they were ready to move to a coop of their own.

'They can move to Cooper's Cottage for a little while,' Maggie suggested to Kate. 'Give Hettie some time to herself. Once you get your school holidays, they can move back here, and you will have plenty of time to rear a flock of your own.'

Hettie's babies were all girls, which meant one thing to Kate. 'When will they lay eggs?'

'Not until they are around five or six months old,' Maggie answered. 'But when they do, you can set up an honesty box of your own.'

'Yes!' said Kate, clapping her hands in glee. Then a worried look crossed her face. 'But won't I be taking your business away?'

'Oh, you are a darling, considerate girl,' said Maggie, giving her a hug. 'There will be plenty of business for all of us!'

Using a calendar, Kate counted down the days until the chicks would start laying eggs of their own. She was excited at the thoughts of having her own egg enterprise.

Soon after her chicks were weaned and living at Cooper's, Hettie started laying eggs again, and when summertime came, Kate knew it was time for the chicks to come back to Hazel Tree. With Dad's help, they created a bigger area to house the growing flock, with new nesting boxes and an extended roost so they could all line up at night-time.

Meanwhile, Larry had thrived under an attentive mother. The children loved to watch him jump and play with the other lambs, especially in the evening when they all seemed to go for one final run before settling in with their mums for some much-needed rest.

However, the biggest success story at Hazel Tree was Blue, who had fully recovered by the time the children got their summer holidays. The weeks of rest had worked wonders, and not just in healing her wounds. Blue was no longer the giddy young dog she had been; she had filled out and now looked stronger and more confident.

She and Peter were back training, and with help from Eamon, they were showing some real progress. Peter had learned his commands and how to use them effectively: 'come bye', 'away to me', 'lie down'.

But that wasn't all Peter had learned!

One day, as he practised his whistling, the usual *prrrrrp-pppphhhhhh* noise was replaced with a low, shrill tune.

'I did it!' he shouted in glee. 'I can whistle!'

With more practice, Peter became such an accomplished whistler that he could do it by putting his two fingers in his mouth and allowing the shrill sound to ring out.

Eamon was proud of the progress Peter and Blue were making, and as July rolled on, he started to think that they might be ready for the Ballynoe Fair after all. But with just a few weeks to go, would they have enough time?

One glorious summer day, Eamon, Peter and Blue stood in the same field where Blue had had her disastrous trial only a few months prior. This morning was to be another test – they had set up gates as if it was a real trial.

Eamon could sense Peter's nerves and knew it was the right time to give him a gift. He handed Peter a dog whistle, the same kind he himself had used with Peg. It was shaped like a triangle and had a long red cord hanging from it.

'All good herdsmen have one of these,' he said. 'It can be tricky to get the hang of, so don't worry if it takes a bit of time and practice. You just need patience.'

Peter hung the cord around his neck and watched as the whistle shone in the summer sun. Following Eamon's instructions, he picked it up and placed it flat against his tongue, covering the lower half with his lips. With the front pointing from his mouth, Peter blew gently. He wasn't sure if it was strong enough or even if this technique was correct …

Phweeeeeeeeeeee!

The piercing sound startled everyone. Blue stood to attention.

'I did it!' Peter gasped. 'And on my first attempt!'

'Hummph,' grunted Eamon, 'beginners' luck.'

Phweeeeeeeeeeee came the sound once again, and Peter's eyes shone with glee.

'All right, all right,' joked Eamon. 'You're a natural.'

Suddenly a look of fear washed over Peter. 'Do you really think I can do this?' he asked Eamon, his voice trembling.

'No,' said Eamon, putting a hand on his shoulder. 'I think *we* can do this.'

* * *

Peter now took a step forward, away from Eamon. He fiddled nervously with his whistle as Eamon gave him some last-minute instructions. This time, it wasn't Eamon taking the lead, it was Peter.

Despite his fears, Peter knew that Eamon believed in him, and in Blue. Their training over the past few weeks, although light, had gone well. Blue's old habits were still there, but Peter was learning how to correct and teach the young dog.

Eamon stood back, leaving Peter and Blue together. He knew that his role from now on was to mentor. To watch and observe. To help only when he was needed, or when his young apprentice called on him. It was important that Blue heard the commands from her master. Their bond was strong, and Blue's instincts had been formed on the night of the vixen attack.

They had all come a long way since their first practice trial just three months before, but Eamon knew how nerve-racking it was to take part in a competitive sheep trial, and he worried that he was expecting too much of young Peter. *I hope I am doing the right thing*, he thought to himself.

'Away to me!' Peter's voice now boomed, lifting Eamon from his nagging thoughts.

As per the command, Blue moved to the right, rounding the sheep and making sure they stayed together.

'Steady ...' Peter's follow-up command made sure that Blue didn't run too much, scattering the group.

Like a crouching lion, her body was low to the ground, her head pointed forward and her stare focused as she concentrated on the job at hand.

'Lie down.' Peter's eyes were focused on Blue as, with one clean motion, she lay down close to the sheep, who were now grouped in the corner hedge. They were still at least five metres from the pen, their destination.

'Come bye!' Peter boomed, moving Blue left to bring the

sheep away from the hedge and back towards the pen.

Without taking her eyes from them, Blue curled her body, rounding the sheep, moving them towards the pen.

'Steady ...' voiced Peter, afraid that they would overshoot the pen and run instead to the far end of the field.

He walked slowly and calmly towards the pen. He needed to get the gate open so Blue could complete the task. It was important he didn't spook the flock or distract her.

'Steady ...' he commanded once again.

Peter reached up to lift the latch of the gate. By now, Blue was not far away, and the sheep were in a perfect formation. It was going well. Blue had done her bit, and now it was down to Peter. His hand shook as he struggled with the latch, which was stuck fast. He wasn't strong enough to release it.

'Come on, come on,' he growled under his breath. 'Please don't do this, not today.'

The sheep were getting closer. If he didn't get the gate open, they would run straight past.

From a distance, Eamon could see Peter was in trouble, but he knew that if he ran over, he would startle the sheep. 'Pull it out and up,' he called out, gesturing to Peter.

But Peter was starting to panic. The latch was well and truly jammed. He tried using both hands, but it was no good. With a final burst of strength, he pulled as hard as he could and his hand slipped, punching him in the face. He fell backwards in a heap on the ground. All he could do was lie there and watch the sheep pass by the pen. Blue ran up to him, licking his face before sitting loyally by his side.

Peter clambered up. He ripped the whistle from around his neck, snapping the cord, and threw it on the ground in a temper. Blue moved away from him, unsure if she was the cause of her master's change of mood.

Eamon ran over, picked up the whistle and gave it back to Peter.

'That was not Blue's fault,' he said. 'It was a human error. We should have made sure our gates were in perfect working order.' He turned to Blue and gave her a rub on her head. 'Good job today, Blue. Sorry we let you down.'

'We were so close,' Peter said in a low voice. 'It was nearly perfect.'

'We learn from the times we fail,' said Eamon. 'Today we learnt how important it is to put grease on gate latches so they work when we need them to. Come on, let's get this job done and give it another go after dinner.'

'Sorry I threw your whistle on the ground,' said Peter, now feeling embarrassed by his behaviour.

Eamon laughed and put his hand on Peter's shoulder. 'You have passion for this, and that's not something to be sorry about. And anyway, it's not *my* whistle, it's *your* whistle.'

* * *

From afar, the vixen watched as the two humans and the dog left the field. She didn't want to get too close in case the dog picked up her scent. She had been lucky that night to get away. It was not in her nature to pick a fight with a dog, but she had no choice – the dog and humans trapped her. Her cubs would not have survived if she hadn't returned to them. She gave up the fight so her cubs could live.

Since her visit, she had not returned to Hazel Tree. Too many risks not worth taking. Lights in the fields and the smell of humans filled the air around. She decided she was no longer on the hunt for lamb and hen – instead, she gave her cubs rabbits and rodents. They had thrived nonetheless, and now it was time for them all to leave the den and find better shelter for the winter that lay ahead. It was nearly time for her cubs to leave her and find their own way in this world. She would not return to Hazel Tree, but the same could not be said about her cubs.

She turned for one final look before disappearing over the hill, her family following close behind.

Chapter Ten

The Big Day

As August arrived, it brought the reminder that cooler days were on their way. But the morning of the Ballynoe Autumn Fair dawned bright and mild. A perfect fair day! The whole town was buzzing with activity. Bunting hung across the lampposts, and shop windows had been painted with festive colours and pictures.

Everyone was in a great mood. Everyone except for Kate.

'What am I going to do?' she grumbled over breakfast, letting clumps of cornflakes slip from her spoon and splash back into the bowl. 'Karen Reilly is entering her hen and chicks into the Best Pet competition. Hettie's chicks aren't cute little fluffballs anymore, and according to my calendar, it'll still be another few weeks before they are laying eggs, so I don't even have anything to show off.'

'Well, you could help me with the judging,' said Mam, taking a sip of her coffee. 'I could really do with an assistant.'

'Assistant judge!' Kate's eyes grew huge at the thought. 'It's like I will be judging the whole class.'

'Well … not exactly,' said Mam, laughing. 'But you will be helping.'

'That's good enough for me,' said a very excited Kate. 'I'd better go get ready. I can't wait to see the look on Karen Reilly's face when I stand there with my clipboard and pen.'

'What clipboard and pen?' asked Mam, but Kate was off, planning her perfect judging outfit and thinking about how it would feel to crown the winners.

＊ ＊ ＊

Peter, meanwhile, knew exactly what he was going to wear. Maggie had made him a suit especially for the occasion: trousers, a matching waistcoat and a peaked cap, just like what Eamon wore back when he did sheep trials with Peg.

'You look so handsome,' Maggie beamed as she pinned up the trouser legs. 'But you will have to stop growing or you'll only get to wear this once!'

The Ballynoe Showgrounds were located outside the village. As Dad pulled in the gate and drove through the grounds, Peter gasped at their size. He had been in the main hall before for the Christmas pantomime and the stadium for sports events, but today was the first time he had seen the showgrounds fully open and in all their glory.

Eamon sat in the front beside Dad, pointing out the direction signs for 'exhibitors' which they followed all the way to the rear of the grounds. There, they saw animal pens and the registration desk. Competition judges were milling about looking very important with their clipboards and 'Judge' badges pinned to their smart suits.

Peter hadn't been feeling nervous earlier, but when they finally parked, he could feel the butterflies in his tummy. He also felt a bit sick. He put his arm around Blue, who was sitting next to him, her tongue lolling and her tail wagging. She licked Peter's face happily. Behind them, the sheep were travelling in the trailer. Peter wondered if they too were feeling a little bit sick, as the journey had been quite bumpy.

The fair wasn't open to the public yet, but the organisers and competitors were busy getting everything ready. Cattle were being washed and groomed for the showing classes, and horses were being exercised and warmed up in the various practice arenas. Some people were walking their dogs, while others were giving them bowls of water. The day was warming up, and these drinks were greeted by happy, wagging tails.

At the entrance to the fair, officials in hi-vis jackets were gathered. One man, seemingly the boss, gave instructions and pointed to different areas. 'No one is to pass this point without a ticket!' he called out. 'It's going to get very busy soon, and you must be at your stations early.'

On arrival, visitors would walk through this area, purchase their tickets and catalogues from one of the booths, and then pass through the turnstiles into the main showgrounds. Once through, they were free to wander to the various arenas to watch the animal showing classes or stroll through the marquees to sample the tasty treats, view the arts and crafts, or look at the winning pets, cakes and flower arrangements. There was a retail village, a farmers' market and a food court with an area set up for cookery demonstrations. Some of the officials were already tucking into breakfast and sipping coffee, filling their bellies before it got too busy.

From the back, Peter caught the sweet aroma of chocolate crêpes and candy floss. Normally he would be dreaming about food, but he was too nervous to think about eating. Every time he looked over to the main arena, his stomach lurched another bit.

Dad noticed his son's pained expression. 'Why don't you and Blue go and get yourselves registered?' he suggested.

'You can check out the arena on your way back,' added Eamon. He hoped that seeing the arena up close might help ease Peter's nerves.

Ballynoe Arena stood like a crown jewel in the centre of the showgrounds. There was a large spectator stand encircling it, with a white fence between the public and the competitors. At one end, three flagpoles stood tall with the Ballynoe colours flapping in the early autumn breeze. At the other end, a large TV screen captured the action for those sitting at the back.

Peter could see two men putting together the pens where the sheep would be herded later that day. Another was watering the flower displays around the edge, while two more were hanging the sponsor's logos at the entrance.

'Watch yourself, young man,' a burly chap called out as he struggled past with a large sign. Then he paused what he was doing and took a closer look at Peter and Blue. 'Are you here for the trials later?' he asked.

Peter nodded, patting Blue as he did so.

'That's a fine-looking dog you have,' the man answered, stepping back to get a better look at Blue.

'It would want to be,' commented another man, on hearing their conversation. 'I believe Malachy McConnell and his dog Jess are taking part. Malachy's already a county champion and no doubt his Jess is another champ in the making. I wouldn't want to be going up against them anyway.'

Seeing the look of dismay on Peter's face, the man with the sign hushed his friend. 'Oh, I don't know, Albert,' he said, smiling at Peter. 'There's always room for new talent in Ballynoe, and maybe this is the year for a new champ.'

Trying to smile, Peter said goodbye and made his way back to Dad. He was clutching a piece of paper with his competition number on it: 104.

Going up against the county champion, he thought, the butterflies in his tummy starting to flutter once again.

* * *

Meanwhile, over in the marquees, the Cakes & Bakes competition was about to begin. The judging always took place before the fair so the judges could spend time inspecting, examining and tasting all the entries. They also got to speak to the excited competitors about their creations.

Maggie had truly outdone herself. Motivated by her fury at Monica Reilly, she had created an entire farmyard out of sponge cake. Homemade biscuits had been drizzled in chocolate to create a ploughed field. Hens sat on sugared almond eggs, while sheep with candy floss wool grazed happily in fields of green icing. The entire scene was surrounded by a candy stick fence.

'Absolutely wonderful,' gushed Freddy Flynn, Maggie's favourite chef and the guest judge on the day. 'Just wonderful. And how lovely to see you again, Maggie.'

Maggie beamed from ear to ear.

Freddy carefully cut a slice from the back of the farmyard and took a small bite. 'As light as a cloud,' he remarked. 'How can I get you to share that recipe with me, Maggie?'

By now, Maggie was positively glowing. 'Oh, that recipe is very special and unique, I couldn't possibly share it,' she exclaimed loudly, so that everyone would hear.

Further down the line of competitors was Monica Reilly. She glared at Maggie's entry, knowing her Fairy Castle couldn't compare. The chocolate biscuit cake walls were doing fine, but the heads of her sugared fairies were looking a little crooked and the lemonade moat had sprung a leak.

It was no surprise to anyone when the judges announced Maggie Cooper as the overall winner.

As Monica clutched her Highly Commended ribbon and took a closer look at Maggie's glorious farmyard, she realised the time had come to end their squabble. She couldn't compete against such an accomplished baker as Maggie Cooper. 'Well done, Maggie,' she said, a little gloomily.

'Why, thank you, Monica,' Maggie replied, taken aback by how courteous Monica was being.

'Mine didn't go quite to plan,' Monica added. 'Maybe you could give me some pointers.'

Was this a trick? Maggie wasn't quite sure, but Monica's expression seemed genuine. Her frostiness melted. 'I'd be happy to! And maybe you could show me your chocolate biscuit cake. I can never get mine quite right.'

'Of course!' said a delighted Monica.

The two ladies smiled at each other, the hatchet finally buried after all these years.

In the neighbouring marquee, Mam and Kate were busy judging the entries in the Best Pet competition. Wearing a beret and a smart jacket, Kate had made herself a badge with 'Judge' written in block letters, which she pinned squarely on the front of her jacket so everyone could see. She made sure to click her pen and tap her clipboard as she strolled up and down the rows of animals. Mam tried to hide her smile as she watched her daughter.

The Best Pet competition had lots of different categories, and Mam had created a scoring sheet for each. The animals would get points for the gloss of their fur (or feathers), the shine in their eyes, and how well they performed in the talent part. Kate was giving extra points for cuteness.

'The shine on their bodies lets us know they're in good condition,' Mam whispered to Kate.

There were all kinds of pets taking part. Kate giggled at the puppies who tugged at her jacket and the cats who purred when she tickled their chins. There was one gerbil who kept running around his wheel until Kate felt dizzy. There was also a goldfish who just hid behind the rock in his bowl.

'Come on, Fluffy,' said his exasperated owner, but to no avail – Fluffy was just feeling too shy to be on show.

Mam announced the winner of the first category. 'Congratulations to Frankie the poodle, winner of Most Talented Pet!'

Kate went next. 'Congratulations to Jimmy the gerbil, winner of the Shiniest Coat!'

The other competitors applauded as each delighted owner

walked up to collect their ribbon. They let out a big cheer as the owner of Fluffy the goldfish took home the Best Gills award.

However, it couldn't be denied that Karen Reilly's hen and chicks were the stars of the show. The three yellow fluffballs happily chirped around their mother, who sat calmly and clucked gently. Kate gave them full marks, and Mam agreed that they should get the overall prize of Best in Show.

'Thank you, thank you!' squealed a delighted Karen.

'You deserve it,' said Kate.

'Hens are my absolute favourites,' said Karen. 'I want to know everything about them.'

'Maybe Karen would like to visit us one day,' said Mam. 'Why don't you invite her, Kate?'

The two girls smiled at each other, excited at the prospect of a play date where they could talk about hens and animals all day long.

* * *

With their work over, Mam and Kate met up with Maggie, who was still clutching her winner's ribbon. It was a very happy trio that headed over to the main arena, where the sheepdog trials were due to begin. As they took their seats, Kate wondered how Dad, Eamon and Peter were feeling.

Over in the staging area, Dad was struggling to pin Peter's

competition number onto his back. 'Stop wriggling, Peter!' he said, exasperated.

'Don't prod me with that pin!' Peter grimaced.

Once he was ready, Peter joined Eamon at the side of the arena, where they could watch the other entries. Only two people were allowed to stay, so Dad gave his son a final hug. 'Best of luck, Peter,' he whispered. 'You've done so well getting here. I am so proud of you and Blue.'

As Peter watched him leave to join the others in the spectator seats, there was a small lump in his throat and butterflies in his tummy. But this was no time for nerves. Eamon had been closely observing what was happening in the ring – or *not* happening, for that matter – and he filled Peter in once he arrived.

Many of the competitors weren't doing at all well. One dog, chased by an angry sheep, had run to hide behind its owner, while another ran out of the ring altogether, snatching a sandwich from one of the spectators on the way.

As this was a trial for young dogs, many of the canine competitors were in a ring for the first time and finding it quite overwhelming. The course, however, was relatively straightforward – the aim was to show what the dog would do on any normal working day at home. A series of 'drive gates' were set up, and the dog needed to guide the sheep through each gate, then in a full circle around to the final holding pen. The dog's master stayed at his or her post until the flock was nearing the pen, then they would come over and close the gate behind the animals, signalling the end of their round.

Yelp!

Peter's attention was brought back by the howl of a dog getting trod on by a sheep. The dog lifted its paw sadly and looked over to its master.

'Competitor 102, Michael Grimes, has retired due to injury,' the commentator's voice crackled over the speaker.

The crowd clapped in both sympathy and appreciation as Michael and his limping dog, Flo, left the arena.

'Oh no,' said Mam, watching from the stands. 'I'd better check that poor girl later.'

Dad arrived and sat down beside her. Mam, Kate and Maggie all looked at him. 'He's feeling nervous,' Dad said, before they could even ask.

The trial was scored out of one hundred. For every mistake that was made, the judges deducted points. So far, the highest anyone got was a fifty-five.

'This is not going well,' muttered Kate. 'I would hate to be judging this.'

'The judges are tough,' said Dad. 'They are looking for a talented and obedient dog as well as a handler who is confident in their commands. The dog has to leave its handler to fetch the sheep, then control them as it moves the flock back.'

'Simple,' remarked Kate. 'Blue can do all those things.'

'Yes,' said Dad, 'but this is a big arena, and Blue must move pretty far away from Peter to reach the flock.'

'Not to mention the final and most important part,' added Maggie, 'when they have to work together to move the sheep into that small pen.'

Kate took in the size of the arena. It was certainly bigger than the field Peter had been practising in, and between the crowds of people and the noise, there were lots of distractions for a young dog. She closed her eyes. 'You can do it, Peter and Blue,' she whispered. 'Pretend you are back in the field at Hazel Tree.'

* * *

It was almost time for Peter and Blue to take to the arena. Only one competitor was left before them, but it was the hot favourite, Malachy McConnell, with his dog Jess. Eamon stood by Peter's side, careful not to say the wrong thing and risk making him even more nervous.

Malachy had come to Ballynoe today with one mission: to win and represent Ballynoe once again in the county finals. So far, from what he had seen of the other competitors, he was feeling confident that he and Jess would be the victors.

As their names were called out, the crowd cheered and clapped. Malachy lifted his cap and acknowledged the applause from all around him. Then, moving into position at the far corner of the arena, he and Jess set to work.

Peter and Eamon watched closely as Malachy, with great skill, guided Jess through her paces. He was calm and confident, and it was easy to see that Jess completely trusted him. She was working independently of her handler and always seemed to be one step ahead of the flock of four sheep.

Everything was going by the book until, suddenly, one sheep broke away from the flock, startling Jess. For any other handler, it would have been a costly mistake, but not for the experienced and composed Malachy McConnell. He quickly remedied the situation with a shrill whistle, which brought Jess left and the rogue sheep right to re-join the flock.

The crowd gasped in awe.

'That was amazing,' whispered Peter. 'I would never have been able to do that.'

'You and Blue wouldn't have let that sheep break free in the first place,' said Eamon with a wink.

Jess turned the bend, driving the sheep down the final straight and through the last set of gates. They were now heading to the pen, and Malachy walked from his post to the gate to ready it. So as not to disturb his dog, Malachy pulled open the gate while the ever-obedient Jess rounded the sheep and brought them forward.

Aside from the error with the stray sheep, it was a near-perfect performance, which received another huge cheer and applause from the crowd. The judges also showed their appreciation, giving Malachy and Jess a score of 90 out of 100.

Now it was Peter and Blue's turn.

'Best of luck, lad,' Eamon said, laying his strong hand on Peter's shoulder. 'You have nothing to prove here today, just experience to gain.'

Peter was by far the youngest competitor in the trials, and if he and Blue won, he would be the youngest herdsman ever to represent Ballynoe at the county finals. Taking a deep breath, he headed towards the ring. There was no going back now.

Everyone clapped as he and Blue entered the ring. There were whisperings around the stand; many people recognised Blue, who was something of a local celebrity since the night of the vixen attack.

They took their positions at one end of the arena. The sheep were held in the pen at the other end. Peter glanced over at Eamon, who gave him a reassuring nod of his head, letting Peter know it was time for Blue's 'outrun', her first run.

Peter turned his attention to an alert and ready Blue. He gave his first command – 'Away to me!' – hoping that his voice didn't sound too shaky. He was nervous … *really* nervous … and Blue might not heed his words if his voice didn't sound the same.

Around his neck he wore the whistle Eamon had given him. It comforted him to know it was there – in a way, he felt like Eamon was standing by his side.

'Come on, lad,' whispered Eamon on the sidelines. 'You can do this.'

'Steady …' Peter's next command was better, stronger, as he fought to overcome his nerves.

Blue heeded her young master, slowing down as she reached the flock, which had now gathered and were awaiting their next move.

'Away to me,' Peter called again. Blue ran in a curve, gathering the flock in a tight group to move through the first set of gates. Her front paws crossed over as she moved in around them, never taking her eyes from the sheep.

'That's it, girl,' mouthed Eamon with a growing sense of confidence.

Suddenly one sheep went to dart away from the gathered flock. This could be disastrous. Without a moment's hesitation, Peter reached for his whistle, placing it against his tongue. The sound rang around the arena. Blue tensed, her senses heightened and her instincts called to the fore.

'Come bye, come bye,' Peter called, and Blue listened, moving quickly and cleanly to stop the stray before any damage could be done.

The move drew a gasp from the crowd, many of whom sat up to take more notice and get a better view. Also watching carefully was Malachy McConnell, who, prior to this development was already celebrating his victory. His focus was now fully on this impressive young duo.

The sheep, all together now, moved seamlessly through the gates.

'That dog really trusts its young master,' said a man sitting in the row in front of Kate, her parents and Maggie. Kate sat up straight, full of pride for her older brother and Blue.

Unaware of the crowd's growing admiration, Peter took a deep breath as he quickly judged the distance between the flock and the final pen. He knew this trial was not about speed – the winner wouldn't be the one who brought the flock in the fastest, but whoever did it with the greatest skill and the least errors. But if he was too slow and went over the allotted time, he would be penalised heavily. The pen was close, and he could easily have the sheep in place within three moves – but only if he got the commands right, and if Blue responded to them correctly.

Blue was now driving the flock around the bend in line with the final set of gates.

'He's doing the cross drive,' muttered Maggie.

'What?' cried Kate. 'What's a cross drive, Dad?'

'It's the part of the competition where the flock will be moved across the field to the next set of gates,' Dad answered, then looked over at Maggie. 'That's right, isn't it?' he asked out the side of his mouth.

Maggie gave him a thumbs up.

Blue's body was now curved, and she criss-crossed her front legs to keep that position. The sheep rounded the final bend in the same curved shape, before straightening out and moving towards the gates.

The crowd was so quiet you could hear a pin drop. It felt as if simply breathing would be too loud.

Kate moved in closer to her mother, who moved in closer to Dad.

'I don't think I can watch,' Mam whispered under her breath.

'Me neither,' whispered Maggie from behind her scarf.

Once again, the sheep passed through the gate in a controlled and steady fashion. All that was left now was to get them to their final destination. This was Peter's cue to leave his post and move towards the gate of the pen. He had watched Malachy McConnell move in a slow and steady motion, never distracting Jess from her role – he would do the same for Blue. She was getting closer, and it was vital not to stop her while she was in motion.

Peter's hand shook as he lifted and pulled back the bolt on the closed gate. As if sitting on air, the bolt slid effortlessly, releasing the gate. With the greatest of care, Peter walked the gate open, gliding it along the grass.

Blue's ears pricked. Her senses once again heightened – she knew now what she must do.

'Steady …' Peter mouthed to Blue.

'Steady …' Eamon said under his breath.

'Steady …' Mam and Dad said together.

'Is it over?' said Maggie from behind her scarf.

'Nearly,' answered Kate from behind Mam.

The gap between the flock and the open pen got smaller. Blue stayed tight to the sheep at the back, ready in case one moved out of line. It was as if she was pushing them forward like links on a chain. After the first sheep entered the pen, the rest dutifully followed.

Blue stood in the gap, making sure none of the flock attempted a last-minute dash. She kept her stare on them, her head lowered and her shoulder blades high. She remained there until Peter had the gate almost fully pulled across. When there was just enough room for her to exit, she stepped back and stood obediently at the rail, waiting for the 'click' which signalled that the bolt was back in position. Once the gate was secured, she sat back, ears pricked and tongue out, looking at the flock now safely secured in their pen.

Peter looked down at Blue, and Blue looked up at Peter. Her tail wagged, and a smile shone across Peter's face.

The crowd erupted.

Mam, Dad and Kate jumped up and down. Eamon threw his cap in the air, and Maggie sobbed into her scarf.

'What a team,' said Malachy McConnell from the sideline.

'Best talent I've seen for quite some time.'

Peter ran over to Eamon and threw himself into his arms. A very excited Blue jumped up and down, barking and wagging her tail in delight.

'We did it, Eamon!' Peter cried out. 'We did it!'

'*You* did it, lad!' Eamon said, hugging Peter tight. 'And Miss Blue, you are every bit as good, if not better, than your mum.'

Peter looked up, hardly able to believe what he had just heard.

Silence fell over the crowd as the judges prepared to deliver their scores. The lead judge stood and turned the score pad to the crowd: *Competitor 104, Peter Farrelly and Blue of Hazel Tree Farm … 95*!

150

Peter and Blue were engulfed once again in Eamon's enormous embrace. In the distance, Peter could see his family in the crowd. Kate was squealing, jumping up and down in delight, and Mam and Dad were waving at him. Maggie was dotting her eyes with her scarf.

Eamon continued to squeeze him, and if it hadn't been for Malachy McConnell coming up to shake Peter by the hand, they would probably still be there.

'You have a natural talent, young man,' Malachy said, 'and that dog of yours is a champion, no doubt about it.'

'That she is,' said Eamon, bursting with pride. 'That she is.'

'You must let me know if she is ever to have a litter of puppies,' added Malachy. 'After today's performance, her pups will be in big demand.'

As they stood in for the winner's photo, Peter made sure that Eamon was holding the cup with him. He could never have done this without Eamon's help. Mam, Dad, Kate and Maggie squeezed in from the side, while Peter laughed at Blue, who was too busy chasing her tail and barking to sit still.

'Cheeeeeese!' cried the photographer as he finally managed to get a photo.

'Mmmmmm, cheese,' thought Peter, suddenly feeling hungry. Very hungry!

It had been a truly amazing day, and the journey home was one of joy and celebration. Maggie and Eamon were squashed into Maggie's tiny car, as cakes, buns, bread and potted plants took up the entire back seat. Maggie clutched her winner's ribbon and balanced her bouquet of flowers on her knee as she listened to Eamon relaying his thoughts on the day's events.

'I knew that Blue had it in her,' he said.

Maggie threw him a side look that said she believed otherwise.

'Well, I *did*!' Eamon tried again.

'Eamon Cooper,' said Maggie with a smile, 'don't you dare tell fibs to me. You had poor Blue written off before she even had a chance to shine. It was the strong bond and instincts that made Peter and Blue champions today. The kind of bond and instincts I have only ever seen once before.'

'When?' asked Eamon. 'Who?'

'Who do you think?' laughed Maggie. 'You and Peg, that's who.'

'Aye,' said Eamon. 'Peg was the best dog I ever had.'

Meanwhile in the back of Dad's jeep, Peter and Kate were clutching the biggest ice-cream cones they could get. The sugar was taking effect, and they chatted away excitedly. Blue was getting loads of cuddles and her fair share of ice cream when the children weren't looking.

'It's called a Smart Cone,' Peter told his sister. 'You can choose whatever flavour or topping you want just by using your voice or blinking your eyes.'

'That sounds like the best dream ever,' Kate said with a sigh, trying to catch the trickles of ice cream as they ran down the cone and reached her fingertips.

'You know I heard something today,' Dad said, turning to Mam, 'about alpacas.'

'Alpacas?' Mam asked suspiciously.

'Yeah,' said Dad. 'Alpacas, seemingly they are great for protecting sheep and keeping foxes out.'

'Is that so …' said Mam, a knowing smile spreading across her face.

'Think we should get one?' said Dad. 'What do you think?'

'Just the one?' said Mam. 'I think we should get two.'

'Yes,' said Dad, delighted. 'Let's get two, and they'd be company for each other.'

Peter's trophy stood proudly between his parents' seats. He couldn't wait to get it engraved, so his name and Peg's would be alongside those of Malachy McConnell, Eamon Cooper and Peg for many years to come.

Ballynoe Champions, Young Dog Trials – the words ran across the shining silver.

'Maybe we'll be county champions some day,' Peter said

dreamily as he turned to Blue, placing his head against hers.

'I love you, Blue,' he whispered. 'You're the bestest, bravest dog there is.'

With a wag of her tail, Blue gave her young master a gentle lick on the face before stealing another bit of his giant ice-cream cone.

obrien.ie/hazel-tree-farm

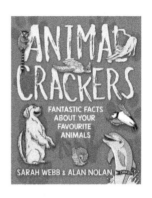
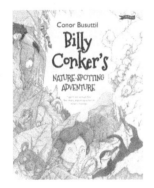

To find out about all our wonderful books
for younger readers, visit **obrien.ie**

Irish Farm Animals

By Glyn Evans and Bex Sheridan

From cows, sheep, donkeys, goats
and chickens to alpacas, rhea
and rare-breed pigs. Discover
everything you need to know
about life on the Irish farm.

The Great Big Book
of Irish Wildlife

By Juanita Browne and Barry Reynolds

A beautiful picture book following
nature through the seasons in Ireland,
from the familiar to weird and
wonderful natural phenomena.

Growing up with

tots to teens and in between

Why CHILDREN love O'Brien:

Over 350 books for all ages, including
picture books, humour, fiction, true stories,
nature and more

Why TEACHERS love O'Brien:

Hundreds of activities and teaching guides,
created by teachers for teachers,
all FREE to download from obrien.ie

Visit, explore, buy
obrien.ie